D0762067

A FAMILY AFFAIR

A NERO WOLFE NOVEL

rex stout

a family affair

THE VIKING PRESS  NEW YORK

A FAMILY AFFAIR

1

WHEN SOMEONE pushes the button at the front door of the old brownstone, bells ring in four places: in the kitchen, in the office, down in Fritz's room, and up in my room. Who answers it depends on the circumstances. If it's ten minutes to one at night and I'm out, no one does unless it won't give up. If it keeps going, say for fifteen minutes, Fritz rolls out, comes up, opens the door the two inches the chain permits, and says nothing doing until morning. If I'm home *I* roll out, open a window and look down to see who it is, and deal with the problem.

It doesn't often ring at that hour, but it did that Monday night —Tuesday morning—late in October. I was home, but not up in bed. I was in the office, having just got in from taking Lily Rowan home after a show and a snack at the Flamingo. I always look in at the office to see if Wolfe has written anything on the pad on my desk. That night he hadn't, and I was crossing to the safe to check that it was locked when the bell rang, and I went to the hall and through the one-way glass of the front door saw Pierre Ducos on the stoop.

Pierre had often fed me. He had fed many people, in one of the three rooms upstairs at Rusterman's restaurant. I had never seen him anywhere else—certainly never on that stoop in the middle of the night. I slipped the bolt back, opened the door, and said, "I'm not hungry, but come in."

He crossed the sill and said, "I've got to see Mr. Wolfe."

"At this hour?" I shut the door. "Not unless it's life and death."

"It is."

"Even so." I looked at him. I had never seen him without his uniform. I knew his age, fifty-two, but he looked older in a loose-fitting tan topcoat down to his knees. No hat. He looked as if inside of the topcoat he had shrunk, and his face looked smaller and seamier. "Whose life and death?"

"Mine."

"You can tell me about it." I turned. "Come along."

He followed me to the office. When I offered to take his coat he said he would keep it on, which was sensible, since the heat had been off for two hours, and we had lowered the thermostat four degrees to save oil. I moved up one of the yellow chairs for him and sat at my desk and asked him what it was.

He gestured with both hands. "It's what you said. Life and death. For me. A man is going to kill me."

"That won't do. Good waiters are scarce, and anyway you're not old enough to die. Who is he, and why?"

"You make it a joke. Death is not a joke."

"Sure it is. It's life that's not a joke. Who's going to kill you?"

"I'll tell Mr. Wolfe."

"He's in bed asleep. He sees people only by appointment, but for you he would make an exception. Come at eleven in the morning. Or if it's urgent, tell me."

"I—" He looked at me. Since he had seen me at close quarters at least fifty times, maybe a hundred, surely he had me sized up, so he may not have been considering me, but he was deciding something for at least ten seconds. He opened his mouth and shut it, then opened it again to speak. "You see, Mr. Goodwin, I know Mr. Wolfe is the greatest detective in the world. Felix says he is—not only Felix, everybody does. Of course you're a good detective too, everybody knows that too, but when a man is sure he's going to be killed unless he—unless . . ." His hands on his knees were fists, and he opened them, palms up. "I've just got to tell Mr. Wolfe."

"Okay. Eleven o'clock tomorrow morning. What time do you go to work?"

"I won't go tomorrow." He looked at his wristwatch. "Just ten hours. If I could—there on that couch? I won't need covers or anything. I won't disturb anything. I won't make any noise."

So he was really wide open, or thought he was. The couch, in the corner beyond my desk, was perfectly sleepable, as I knew from experience, having spent quite a few nights on it in emergencies, and on the other side of the projecting wall that made the corner was an equipped bathroom. But leaving anyone loose all night in the office, with the ten thousand items in the files and drawers, many of them with no locks, was of course out of the question. There were four alternatives: persuade him to tell me, go up and wake Wolfe, give him a bed, or bounce him. The first might take an hour, and I was tired and sleepy. The second was inadvisable. If I bounced him, and he couldn't come at eleven in the morning because he was dead, the next time Wolfe lunched or dined in the little upstairs room at Ruster-man's he would be served by a new waiter, and that would be regrettable. Also, of course, I would be sorry.

I looked at him. Should I frisk him? Was there any chance that he had it in for Wolfe personally for some reason unknown to me, or that he had been hired by one of the thousand or so people who thought it would be a better world with no Nero Wolfe? Of course it was possible, but if so, this complicated stunt wasn't the way to do it. It would have been much simpler and surer for Pierre just to put something in a sauce, in anything, the next time Wolfe went there for a meal. Anyway, not only had Pierre seen me at close quarters; I had seen him.

I said, "My pajamas would be too big for you."

He shook his head. "I'll keep my clothes on. Usually I sleep with nothing on."

"All right, there's plenty of cover on the bed in the South Room. It's two flights up, on the same floor as my room, above

Mr. Wolfe's room. I was on my way up when you rang the door-bell." I stood. "Come along."

"But Mr. Goodwin, I don't want— I can just stay here." He stood up.

"No, you can't. Either you go up or you go out."

"I don't want to go out. Sunday night a car tried to run over me. He tried to kill me. I'm *afraid* to go out."

"Then follow me. Maybe when you sleep on it . . ."

I moved, crossed to the door, and he came. I flipped the light switch. I don't dawdle going upstairs, and I had to wait for him at the top of the first flight because he was only halfway up. At the second landing I turned left, swung the door of the South Room open, and turned the light on. I didn't have to check on the bed or towels in the bathroom because I knew everything was in order; all I had to do was turn the radiator on.

"I'm sorry, Mr. Goodwin," he said. "I'm very sorry."

"So am I," I said. "I'm sorry you're in a jam. Stick right here until I tell you I've told Mr. Wolfe about you. That will be around nine o'clock. If you open the door and go into the hall before eight o'clock, it will set off a gong in my room and you'll see me coming with guns in both hands. Security. I should have offered you a shot of something. Whisky? Would it help you go to sleep?"

He said no and he was sorry, and I went, shutting the door. As I entered my room, down the hall, I looked at my watch. Seventeen minutes past one. I wouldn't get my eight hours. When I get in that late I usually set my radio-alarm at nine-thirty, but now that wouldn't do. I would have to be up and dressed and telling Wolfe about the company before he went up to the plant rooms at nine o'clock.

Of course I have figured how many minutes had passed after I entered my room when it happened. Six, possibly seven. I refuse to hurry the night routine. I had got my pajamas from the closet, set the alarm, put things from my pockets on the dresser, turned the bedcovers down, turned the telephone and other two switches on, hung up my jacket and necktie, taken my shoes and socks off, and was unbuckling my belt, when the earthquake came and the house shook. Including the floor I was standing on. I have since tried to decide what the sound was like and couldn't. It wasn't like thunder or any kind of gun or any other sound I had ever heard. It wasn't a thud or a bang or a boom; it was just a loud noise. Of course there were doors and walls between it and me.

I jumped to the door and opened it and turned the hall light on. The door to the South Room was shut. I ran to it and turned the knob. No. He had bolted it. I ran down one flight, saw that the door to Wolfe's room was intact, and went and knocked on it. My usual three, a little spaced. I really did, and his voice came.

"Archie?"

I opened the door and entered and flipped the light switch. I don't know why he looks bigger in those yellow pajamas than in clothes. Not fatter, just bigger. He had pushed back the yellow electric blanket and black sheet and was sitting up.

"Well?" he demanded.

"I don't know," I said, and I hope my voice didn't squeak from the pleasure of seeing him. "I put a man in the South Room. The door's bolted. I'm going to see."

Of the three windows in the south wall, the two end ones are always open at night about five inches, and the middle one is shut and locked and draped. I went and pulled the drape, slid the catch, opened it, and climbed through. The fire escape is only a foot wider than the window. I have tried to remember if my bare feet felt the cold of the iron grating as I went up but can't. Of course they didn't when I got high enough to see that most of the glass in the window was gone. I put my hand in between the jagged edges and slipped the catch and pushed the window up, what was left of it, and stuck my head in.

He was on his back with his head toward me and his feet toward the closet door in the right wall. I shoved some glass slivers off the windowsill, climbed through, saw no pieces of glass on the rug, and crossed to him. He had no face left. I had never seen anything like it. It was about what you would get if you pressed a thick slab of pie dough on a man's face and then squirted blood on the lower half. Of course he was dead, but I was squatting to make sure when something hit the door three hard knocks, and I went and slid the bolt and opened it and there was Wolfe. He keeps one of his canes in the stand in the downstairs hall and the other four on a rack in his room, and he was gripping the biggest and toughest one with a knob the size of my fist, which he says is Montenegrin applewood.

I said, "You won't need that," and sidestepped to give him room.

He crossed the sill, stood, and sent his eyes around.

I said, "Pierre Ducos, Rusterman's. He came just after I got home and said a man was going to kill him and he had to tell you. I said if it was urgent he could tell me or he could come and tell you at eleven o'clock. He said a car had tried to run him down and—"

"I want no details."

"There aren't any. He wanted to wait for you there on the couch, and of course that wouldn't do, so I brought him up here and told him to stay put and went to my room, and in a few minutes I felt it and heard it and went. He had bolted the door, and—"

"Is he dead?"

"Yes. The windows blew out, to the outside, so it was a bomb. I'll take a look before I call for help. If you—"

I stopped because he was moving. He crossed to Pierre, bent over, and looked. Then he straightened and looked around, at the closet door, which had been standing open and had hit the wall and was split, at the ceiling plaster on the floor, at the table wrong side up and the pieces of the lamp that had been on it, at the chair that had been tossed clear across to the foot of the bed, and so on.

He looked at me and said, "I suppose you had to."

That remark has since been discussed at length, but then I merely said, "Yeah. I'm going to—"

"I know what you're going to do. First put your shoes on. I am going to my room and bolt the door. I will stay there until they have come and gone and I will see no one. Tell Fritz that when he brings my breakfast he will make sure that no one is near. When Theodore comes, tell him not to expect me. Is there anything you *must* say?"

"No."

He went, still gripping the Montenegrin applewood by the small end. I didn't hear the elevator, so he took the stairs, which he rarely does. Barefoot.

He had *not* known what I was going to do. He hadn't known that I would go down to the basement, to Fritz's room. First I went and put on socks and shoes and a jacket, then down two flights to the office to turn the thermostat up to 70, and then on down to knock on Fritz's door and call my name, loud. He's a sound sleeper, but in half a minute the door opened. The tail of his white nightshirt flapped in the breeze from the open window. Our pajamas-versus-nightshirt debate will never be settled.

"Sorry to intrude," I said, "but there's a mess. A man came, and I put him in the South Room, and a bomb that he brought along went off and killed him. All the damage is in that room. Mr. Wolfe came up for a look and is now in his room with the door bolted. You may not get much more sleep, because a mob will be coming and there will be noise. When you take his breakfast up—"

"Five minutes," he said. "You'll be in the office?"

"No. Upstairs. South Room. When you take his breakfast, be sure you're alone."

"Four minutes. Do you want me upstairs?"

"No. Down. You can let them in, that'll help. There's no rush. I have a couple of chores before I call them."

"Who do I let in?"

"Anybody. Everybody."

"*Bon Dieu.*"

"I agree." I turned and headed for the stairs and on the way up decided not to get rubber gloves from the office because they would make it take longer.

He was still on the floor, and the first question was what had put him there. I couldn't qualify as an expert on that, but I might get an idea, and I did. Here and there among the pieces of plaster on the floor I found several small objects that hadn't come from the ceiling, which I couldn't name. The biggest one was about half the size of my thumbnail. But I found four that I might name, or thought I might—four little pieces of aluminum. The biggest one was a quarter of an inch wide and nearly half an inch long, and EDR was printed on it, dark green. A smaller one had DO printed on it, and another one had *du*. One had no printing. I left them there, where I found them. The trouble with removing evidence from the scene of a crime is that someday you might want to produce it and have to tell where you got it.

The second question was what had made me consider rubber gloves: was there anything on him that would supply a name or other fact? I got on my knees beside him and did a thorough job. He still had the topcoat on, but there was nothing in the pockets. In the jacket and pants pockets were most of the usual items—cigarettes, matches, a couple of dollars in change, key ring, handkerchief, penknife, wallet with driving license and credit cards and eighty-four dollars in bills—but nothing that offered any hope of a hint. Of course there were other possibilities, his shoes or something taped to his hide, but that would take time, and I had already stretched it.

I went down to the office, and Fritz was there, fully dressed. I sat at my desk, pulled the phone around, and dialed a number I didn't have to look up.

2

THE ATTITUDE of Sergeant Purley Stebbins toward Wolfe and me is yes-and-no, or make it no-but-yes. When he finds us within ten miles of a homicide, he wishes he was on traffic or narcotics, but he knows that something will probably happen that he doesn't want to miss. My attitude toward him is that he could be worse. I could name a few that are.

At 4:52 a.m. he sat on one of the yellow chairs in the office, swallowed a bite he had taken from a tongue sandwich made with Fritz's bread, and said, "You know damn well I have to ask him if Ducos or anyone at the restaurant has ever said anything that could be a lead. Or someone does. Someone will come either at eleven o'clock or six."

I had finished my sandwich. "I doubt if he'll get in," I said. "Certainly not at eleven, and probably not at six. He may not be speaking even to me. A man murdered here in his house, within ten feet of him? You know him, don't you?"

"Do I. So does the inspector. I know you too. If you think you can—"

I slapped my desk with a palm. "Don't start that again. I said in my signed statement that I went over him. There might have been something that I should have included when I phoned. But I took nothing. One thing that's not in my statement: I admit I'm withholding evidence. Knowledge of something that would certainly be used at the trial, if and when."

"Oh. You are. You *are?*"

"I am. Of course you'll send everything you found to the lab, and it won't take them long to get it, maybe a couple of days. But you might like to have the pleasure of supplying it yourself. I know what the bomb was in."

"You do. And didn't put it in your statement."

"It would have taken about a page, and I was tired, and also I prefer to tell you. Have you ever seen a Don Pedro cigar?"

He finished swallowing the last bite of the sandwich, with his eyes glued to me. "No."

"Cramer wouldn't buy them to chew. Ninety cents apiece. Rusterman's has them. They come in aluminum tubes. DON PEDRO is on the tube in capital letters, dark green, and *Honduras* is on it, lower case. In the stuff you collected is a piece of aluminum with DO in caps on it, and one with *du* in lower case, and a bigger one with EDR in caps. So this is what happened. When I left the room, he sat or stood or walked around for a few minutes and decided he might as well undress and go to bed and went and opened the closet door. When you take your coat off to hang it up, do you automatically stick your hands in the pockets? I do. So did he. And in one of them was a Don Pedro cigar aluminum tube, which of course he recognized. He had no idea how it got there, and he screwed the cap off, holding it fairly close to his face—say ten inches. It was a piece of aluminum that made the gash on his jaw. There's a word for the force that pushed his face in, but I've forgotten it. If you want to include it in your report, you can look it up."

Purley's mouth was shut tight. He didn't open it. His eyes at me were half shut. There was half an inch of milk left in my glass, and I lifted it and drank. "What those pieces of aluminum were—" I said, "I had that figured before I phoned, but the rest of it, where it had been and exactly how it happened—I doped that out later to occupy my mind while I sat around. Also I considered what would have happened if I had frisked him before I took him upstairs. Of course I would have wanted to see what was in the tube. Well. I'm still here. I have explained why I didn't frisk him. Since I left this out of my statement, leaving it for you, you ought to send me a box of candy. I like caramels."

He finally opened his mouth. "I'll send you an orchid. Do you know what would happen if Rowcliff got on this?"

"Certainly. He would send a squad out to dig up where I recently bought a Don Pedro cigar. But you have a brain, which you sometimes use."

"Put *that* in a statement some day. My brain tells me that he might have said something which gave you a hint how the tube got in his pocket, but that's not in your statement."

"I guess I forgot. Nuts."

"Also my brain tells me that the DA will want to know why I didn't bring you down as a material witness. The bomb went off at one-twenty-four, and you were in the room and found him two or three minutes later, and you phoned at two-eleven. Forty-five minutes, and you know what the law says, and you've got a license."

"Must we go back to that again?"

"The DA will want to know why I didn't bring you."

"Sure, and you'll tell him. So will I after I get some sleep. It was obvious that there was no rush. Whatever had killed him, he had brought it himself. It was the middle of the night. If you had got here in two minutes there wasn't a damn thing you could do that wouldn't wait. You can't do anything now until morning, like finding out where he was and who he saw before he came here. There's nobody at Rusterman's but the night watchman, and he's probably asleep. I have a suggestion. Instead of sending me an orchid, give me permission in writing to break the seal on that room and go in and cover the windows with something. It's not sealed anyway. One of the windows, anyone could come up the fire escape and climb in. I admit there's no hurry about the rest of it, the plaster and other stuff."

"The plaster is gone." He looked at his watch and got to his feet, gripping the chair arms for leverage, which he seldom does. "By god, you admit something. You're going soft. That window's blocked. You let that seal alone. Someone will come for another look, someone who knows about bombs. Also someone will come to see Wolfe."

"I told you, he probably won't—"

"Yeah. Do you know what I think? I think he made a hole in his ceiling and pushed the bomb through." He headed for the door.

I got up and followed, in no hurry. There was no hurry left in me. There wasn't much of anything left in me. When he was out and the door shut, I went and put the chain bolt on, put out the lights in the office and hall, and went up the two flights to my room, actually leaving the plates and glasses there on my desk, which is hard to believe. Fritz had gone to bed nearly an hour ago, when all the mob had cleared out except Purley, after bringing sandwiches without asking if they were wanted.

Of course I was asleep two minutes after I got flat, and I stayed asleep. I don't brag about my sleeping because I suspect it shows that I'm primitive or vulgar or something, but I admit it. But I also admit I set the alarm for ten o'clock. Anyway I would probably be interrupted before that, although I turned my phone switch off. I left the house phone on.

But I wasn't. When the radio said, "And you'll never regret that you obeyed the impulse and decided to try the only face cream that makes you want to touch your own skin," I reached for it without opening my eyes. I tried to argue that another hour wouldn't hurt, but it didn't work because it came to me that there was a problem that wouldn't wait. Theodore. I opened my eyes, reached for the house phone, and buzzed the kitchen.

In five seconds Fritz's voice came. "Yes."

He claims that he is not copying Wolfe, that Wolfe says "Yes?" and he says "Yes."

I said, "You're up and dressed."

"Yes. I took his breakfast."

"Did he eat?"

"Yes."

"My god, you're short and sweet."

"Not sweet, Archie. Neither is he. Are you?"

"No. I'm neither sweet nor sour. I'm done. How about Theodore?"

"He came and went up. I told him he wouldn't come."

"I'll be down, but don't bother with breakfast. I'll eat the second section of the *Times*. With vinegar."

"It's better with ketchup." He hung up.

But when I finally made it down to the kitchen the stage was set. Tools and cup and saucer and the toaster and butter dish were on the little table, and the *Times* was on the rack, and the griddle was on the range. On the big center table was a plate of slices of homemade scrapple. I got a glass and went to the refrigerator for orange juice, poured some, and took a sip.

"As far as I'm concerned," I said, "you and I are still friends. You're the only friend I've got in the world. Let's go somewhere. Switzerland? That ought to be far enough. Have there been phone calls?"

"There have been rings, four, but I didn't answer. Neither did he." He had turned the heat on under the griddle. "That thing on the door of that room, NEW YORK POLICE DEPARTMENT, how long will it stay?"

I drank orange juice. "That's a good idea," I said. "Forget all the other details, such as headlines like GUEST IN NERO WOLFE'S HOUSE KILLED BY BOMB or ARCHIE GOODWIN OPENS DOOR TO HOMICIDE, and concentrate on that door. Wonderful idea."

He was getting bacon fat on the griddle. I went to my chair at the little table and picked up the *Times*. President Ford wanted us to do something about inflation. Nixon was in shock from the operation. Judge Sirica had told Ehrlichman's lawyer he talked too much. The Arabs had made Arafat it. Items which ordinarily would have had me turning to inside pages, but I had to use will power to finish the first paragraphs. I tried other departments—sports, weather, obituaries, metropolitan briefs—and decided that it's possible to tell your mind what to do only when your mind agrees with you. I was going on from there to decide if that meant anything and if so what, when Fritz came with two slices of scrapple on a plate. As he put it down he made a noise which I'll spell "Tchahh!" I asked him why, and he said he forgot the honey and went and brought it.

As I was buttering the third slice of toast the phone rang. I counted. It rang twelve times and stopped. In a couple of minutes Fritz said, "I never saw you do that before."

"There'll probably be a lot of things you never saw me do before. Did you get the plates and glasses I left in the office?"

"I haven't been to the office."

"Did he mention me when you took his breakfast up or went for the tray?"

"No. He asked me if I had been up during the night. I started to tell him about it, how many of them had come, and he stopped me."

"How did he stop you?"

"By looking at me and then turning his back."

"Was he dressed?"

"Yes. The dark brown with little stripes. Yellow shirt and brown tie."

When I put the empty coffee cup down and went to the office it was ten past eleven. Since he hadn't come down at eleven, he probably wasn't coming. I decided it would be childish not to do the chores, so I dusted the desks, removed yesterday's calendar sheets, changed the water in the vase on Wolfe's desk, took the plates and glasses to the kitchen, and put the chair Purley had sat on where it belonged, and was opening the mail when the house phone buzzed. I got it and said, "I'm in the office."

"Have you eaten?"

"Yes."

"Come up here."

I got the carbon of my statement from the drawer and went. Since I had been summoned, of course I didn't knock on his door. He was seated at the table between the windows, with a book. Either he had finished with his copy of the *Times* or his mind had refused to cooperate, like mine. As I crossed to him he put the book down—*The Palace Guard* by Dan Rather and Gary Gates—and growled, "Good morning."

"Good morning," I snarled.

"Have you been downtown?"

"No. I don't answer the phone."

"Sit down and report."

Of course he had the big chair. I brought the other one over and sat and said, "The best start would be for you to read this copy of the statement I gave Stebbins." I handed it to him. It was four pages. Once through is usually enough for him, but that time he went back to the first two pages—what Pierre and I had said, which I had given verbatim.

He eyed me. "What did you reserve?"

"Of my talk with Pierre, nothing. Every word is there. Of the rest, also nothing, except that you were armed when you came, with that club, and that you told me you supposed I had to. It's all there, what was said and what happened, but I didn't include a guess I made. I saved that for Stebbins. When I left Pierre there, he felt something in his topcoat pocket and took it out. It was an aluminum tube, the kind Don Pedro cigars come in. When he unscrewed the cap, he was holding it only a few inches from his face. You saw his face. There were pieces of aluminum on the floor, and I recognized the printing on them. Of course they had been collected and Stebbins had seen them. Also of course, they would soon make the same guess, so I thought I might as well give it to Stebbins."

He shook his head, either at Purley or at me, I didn't know which. "What else did you give him?"

"Nothing. There was nothing else to give. Nothing to any-body, including the medical examiner and Lieutenant Burnham, whom you have never met. I didn't count, but Fritz says there were nineteen of them altogether. The door of the South Room is sealed. A bomb specialist is coming to get clues, probably this afternoon."

When he wants to give something a good look and is in the office at his desk, in the one chair that he thoroughly approves, he leans back and shuts his eyes, but the back of that chair isn't the right angle for it, so he just squinted and pulled at his ear lobe. A full two minutes.

"Nothing," he said. "Nothing whatever."

"Right. Because you're the greatest detective in the world. Stebbins doesn't believe it. He thinks he told me something, maybe not a name but something, and I left it out because we want to get him ourselves. Of course we do, at least I do. I might have unscrewed the cap of that tube myself. So I owe him something."

"So do I. In my own house, asleep in my own bed, and that. That—that . . ."

I raised my brows at him. That was a first. The first time in my long experience that he had ever been at a loss for words.

He hit the chair arm with a fist. "So. Call Felix. Tell him we'll be there for lunch." He looked at the wall clock. "In half an hour. If no upstairs room is available, perhaps on the top floor, if that's convenient. Do you know of any source of information about Pierre other than the restaurant?"

I said no, got up, went to the phone on the bedstand, switched it on, and dialed.

3

THE TOP FLOOR at Rusterman's restaurant was once the living quarters of Marko Vukcic, its owner, who had been Wolfe's boyhood friend in Montenegro and one of the only three men I knew who called him by his first name. For a year or so after Marko's death it had been unoccupied, and then Felix, who had been left a one-third share and ran the restaurant under Wolfe's supervision as trustee, had moved in with his wife and two children. Soon the children had got married and left.

At twenty-five minutes to one, Wolfe and I were seated at a table near a window on that floor which looked down on Madison Avenue. Felix, slim and trim, elegant in blue-black and white for the lunch customers, standing at Wolfe's left and my right, said, "Then the scallops. Fresh from the bay, I never saw finer ones, and the shallots were perfect. They'll be ready in ten minutes."

Wolfe nodded. "And the rice fritters. I'll tell—his name is Philip?"

"Philip Correla. Of course everyone knew Pierre, but Philip knew him best. As I said, I don't think I ever saw Pierre except here. We'll miss him, Mr. Wolfe. He was a good man. It's hard to believe, there in your house." He looked at his watch. "You'll excuse me—I'll send Philip." He went. The early ones would be coming down below.

"Uhuh," I said. "A million people will be saying that, it's hard to believe, there in Nero Wolfe's house. Or some of them will say it's easy to believe. I don't know which is worse."

He glared at me.

Of the seventy-some at Rusterman's altogether, there were few that Wolfe had never seen, only seven or eight who had come since he had bowed out as trustee. When Philip Correla appeared, white apron and cap, he crossed to us and said, "You may remember me, Mr. Wolfe. And Mr. Goodwin."

"Certainly," Wolfe said. "You once disagreed with me about *Rouennaise* sauce."

"Yes, sir. You said no bay leaf."

"I nearly always say no bay leaf. Tradition should be respected but not sanctified. I concede that you make good sauces. Will you sit, please? I prefer eyes at a level."

He waited until Philip had moved a chair to face him and was on it. Then: "I presume Felix told you what I want."

"Yes, sir. To ask me about Pierre. We were friends. *Good* friends. I tell you, I cried. In Italy men cry. I didn't leave Italy until I was twenty-four. I met Pierre in Paris." He looked at me. "It said on the radio you found him." He looked at Wolfe. "In your house. It didn't say why he was at your house or why he got killed."

Wolfe took in a bushel of air through his nose and let it out through his mouth. Felix, and now Philip, and they knew him. "He came to ask me something," he said, "but I was in bed. So I don't know what he wanted to ask, and that's why I need information from you. Since you were his friend, since you wept, it may be assumed that you want the man who killed him exposed and punished. Yes?"

"Of course I do. Have you—do you know who killed him?"

"No. I'm going to find out. I want to tell you something in confidence and ask you some questions. You are to tell no one— *no one*. Can you keep it to yourself?"

"Yes, sir."

"Not many people are sure of themselves. Are you?"

"I'm sure I can keep a secret. I'm sure I can keep this kind of a secret."

"Good. Pierre told Mr. Goodwin that a man was going to kill him, but that's all he told him. Had he told you?"

"That a man was going to kill him? No, sir."

"Had he spoken of any threat, any danger impending?"

"No, sir."

"Had he mentioned any recent event, anything done or said by somebody, that might have suggested a possibility of danger?"

"No, sir."

"But you have seen him and spoken with him recently? Yesterday?"

"Of course. I'm in the kitchen, and he's in front, but we usually eat lunch together in the kitchen. We did yesterday. I didn't see him Sunday; of course, we're not here Sunday."

"When did you hear—learn of his death?"

"The radio this morning. The eight-o'clock news."

"Only five hours ago. You were shocked, and there hasn't been much time. You may recall something he said."

"I don't think I will, Mr. Wolfe. If you mean something about danger, about someone might kill him, I'm sure I won't."

"You can't be sure now. Memory plays tricks. This next question is important. He told Mr. Goodwin a man was going to kill him, so something had happened that put him in fear of his life. When? Just last evening? It would help to know when, so this is important. What was he like yesterday at lunch? Was he completely normal? Was there anything unusual about his mood, his behavior?"

"Yes, sir, there was. I was remembering that when you asked if he said anything about danger. He didn't seem to hear things I said and he didn't talk as much. When I asked him if he would rather eat alone he said he was sorry, that he had got orders mixed at lunch and served people wrong. I thought that explained it. Pierre was a very proud man. He thought a waiter should never make a mistake, and he thought he never did. I don't know, maybe he didn't. You can ask Felix. Pierre often mentioned that when you came you always liked to have him. He was proud of his work."

"Had he actually done that? Got orders mixed?"

"I don't know, but he wouldn't have said that if he hadn't. You can ask Felix."

"Did he mention it again later?"

"No, sir. Of course I didn't."

"Had he been like that Saturday? Distraught?"

"I don't—" Philip frowned. "No, sir, he hadn't."

"I suggest that when opportunity offers you sit and close your eyes and try to recall everything he said yesterday. If you do that, make a real effort, you may surprise yourself. People frequently do. Will you do that?"

"Yes, sir, but not here. I couldn't, here. I will later."

"And tell me or Mr. Goodwin."

"Yes, sir."

"Good. We'll hope to hear from you." Wolfe cocked his head. "Now. Another important question. If he was killed by someone who works here, who was it? Who might have had reason to want him dead? Who feared him or hated him or might have profited by his death?"

Philip was shaking his head. "Nobody. Nobody here. Nobody anywhere."

"Pfui. You can't know that. Obviously you can't, since someone killed him."

He was still shaking his head. "No, sir. I mean yes, sir. Of course. But I can't believe it. That's what I thought when I heard it—who could have killed him? Why would anybody kill Pierre? He never hurt anybody, he wouldn't. Nobody hated him. Nobody was afraid of him. He was a fine man, an honest man. He wasn't perfect, he had that one fault, he bet too much on horse races, but he knew he did and he tried to stop. He didn't want to talk about it, but sometimes he did. I was his best friend, but he never tried to borrow from me."

"Did he borrow from anyone?"

"I don't think so. I don't think he would. I'm sure he didn't from anybody here. If he had, there would have been talk. You can ask Felix."

Apparently the idea was that Felix knew everything.

"Did he bet large amounts?"

"I don't really know. He didn't like to talk about it. Once he told me he won two hundred and thirty dollars, and another time a hundred and something, I forget exactly, but he never spoke about losing."

"How did he bet? Bookmakers?"

"I think he used to, but I'm not sure. Then OTB. He told me when he started at OTB."

"OTB?"

"Yes, sir. Off-Track Betting."

Wolfe looked at me. I nodded. The things he doesn't know, and he reads newspapers. He went back to Philip. "Of course you saw him elsewhere, not only here. Have you ever been in his home?"

"Yes, sir. Many times. His apartment on West Fifty-fourth Street."

"With his wife?"

"She died eight years ago. With his daughter and his father. His father had a little bistro in Paris, but he sold it and came over to live with Pierre when he was seventy years old. He's nearly eighty now."

Wolfe closed his eyes, opened them, looked at me and then at the wall, but there was no clock. He got the tips of his vest between thumb and finger, both hands, and pulled down. He didn't know he did that, and I never mentioned it. It was a sign that his insides had decided that it was time to eat. He looked at me. "Questions? About betting?"

"Not about the betting. One question." I looked at Philip. "The number on Fifty-fourth Street?"

He nodded. "Three-eighteen. Between Ninth Avenue and Tenth."

"There will probably be more questions," Wolfe said, "but they can wait. You have been helpful, Philip, and I am obliged. You will be here for dinner?"

"Yes, sir, of course. Until ten o'clock."

"Mr. Goodwin may come. Felix knows about lunch for us. Please tell him we are ready."

"Yes, sir." Philip was up. "You will tell me what you find out." He looked at me and back at Wolfe. "I want to know. I want to know everything about it."

Well, well. You might have thought he was Inspector Cramer. Wolfe merely said, "So do I. Tell Felix to send our lunch." And Philip turned and walked out without saying yes, sir, and I said, "The question is, was it you or me? He probably thinks me."

Whenever he eats at Rusterman's, Wolfe has a problem. There's a conflict. On the one hand, Fritz is the best cook in the world, and on the other hand, loyalty to the memory of Marko Vukcic won't admit that there is anything wrong with anything served at that restaurant. So he passed the buck to me. When about a third of his portion of the baked scallops was down, he looked at me and said, "Well?"

"It'll do," I said. "Maybe a little too much nutmeg, of course that's a matter of taste, and I suspect the lemon juice came out of a bottle. The fritters were probably perfect, but they came in piles and Fritz brings them just three at a time, two to you and one to me. That can't be helped."

"I shouldn't have asked you," he said. "Flummery. Your palate is incapable of judging the lemon juice in a cooked dish."

Of course he was under a strain. Business is never to be mentioned at the table, but since there was no client and no prospect of a fee, this was all in the family and therefore wasn't business, and it was certainly on his mind. Also the waiter wasn't Pierre, whom he would never have again. He was some kind of Hungarian or Pole named Ernest, and he was inclined to tilt things. However, he ate, including the almond parfait, which I had suggested, and had a second cup of coffee. As for conversation, that was no problem. Watergate. He probably knew more about every angle of Watergate than any dozen of his fellow citizens, for instance the first names of Haldeman's grandparents.

He had intended to have another talk with Felix, but as we pushed our chairs back and rose he said, "Can you have the car brought to the side entrance?"

"Now?"

"Yes. We're going to see Pierre's father."

I stared at him. " 'We'?"

"Yes. If you brought him to the office we would be interrupted. Since Mr. Cramer and the District Attorney have been unable to find us, there may already be a warrant."

"I could bring him here."

"At nearly eighty, he may not be able to walk. Also the daughter may be there."

"Parking in the fifties is impossible. There may be three or four flights and no elevator."

"We'll see. Can it be brought to the side entrance?"

I said of course and got his coat and hat. It certainly was all in the family. For a client, no matter how urgent or how big a fee, it had never come to this and never would. He took the elevator in the rear and I took the one in front, since I had to tell Otto where to send the car.

The West Fifties are a mixture of everything from the "21" Club to grimy walkups and warehouses, but I knew that block on Fifty-fourth was mostly old brownstones, and there was a parking lot near Tenth Avenue. When we were in and rolling, I suggested going to the garage and leaving the Heron, which Wolfe owns and I drive, and taking a taxi, but he thinks a moving vehicle with anyone but me at the wheel is even a bigger risk and vetoed it. So I crossed to Tenth Avenue and then uptown, and there was space at the parking lot. Only one long block to walk.

Number 318 wasn't too bad. Some of those brownstones had been done over inside, and that one even had wooden paneling in the vestibule, and a house phone. I pushed the fourth button up, which was tagged Ducos, put the receiver to my ear, and in a minute a female voice said, "Who ees eet?" If it was Pierre's daughter, I thought she should have better manners, but probably she had been given a busy day by a string of city employees and journalists. It was ten minutes past three.

"Nero Wolfe," I told her. "W-O-L-F-E. To see Mr. Ducos. He will probably know the name. And Goodwin, Archie Goodwin. We knew Pierre for years."

"Parlez-vous français?" she said.

I knew that much, barely. "Mr. Wolfe does," I said. "Hold it." I turned. "She said parly voo fransay. Here." He took the receiver, and I moved to make room. He didn't have to stoop quite as much as me to get his mouth at the right level. Since what he said was for me only noise, I spent the couple of minutes enjoying the idea of a homicide dick pushing that button and hearing parly voo fransay, and hoping it was Lieutenant Rowcliff. Also a couple of journalists I had met, especially Bill Wengert of the *Times*. When Wolfe hung up the receiver, I put a hand on the inside door and, when the click sounded, pushed it open. And there was a do-it-yourself elevator with the door standing open.

If you speak French and would prefer to have a verbatim report of Wolfe's conversation with Léon Ducos, Pierre's father, I'm sorry I can't deliver. All I got was an idea of how it was going from their tones and looks. I'll report what I saw. First, at the door of the apartment it wasn't Pierre's sister. She had said good-by to fifty and maybe even sixty. She was short and dumpy, with a round face and a double chin, and she sported a little white apron, and a little white cap thing on top of her gray hair. Probably she spoke English, at least some, but she didn't look it. She took Wolfe's coat and hat and ushered us to the front room. Ducos was there in a wheelchair by a window. The best way to describe him is just to say that he was shriveled but still tough. He probably weighed thirty pounds less than he had at fifty, but what was left of him was intact, and when I took his offered hand I felt his grip. During the hour and twenty minutes we were there he didn't say a word that I understood. Probably he spoke no English at all, and that was why she had asked if I spoke French.

In twenty minutes, even less, their tone and manner had made it plain that no blood would be shed, and I left my chair, looked around, and crossed to a cabinet with a glass door and shelves in the far corner. Most of the shelves had things like little ivory and china figures and sea shells and a wooden apple, but on one there was a collection of inscribed trophies, silver cups and a medal that might have been gold, and a couple of ribbons. The only word on them that I knew was a name, Léon Ducos. Evidently his bistro had done something that people liked. I sent my eyes around, detecting. You do that in the home of a man who has just been murdered, and, as usual, nothing suggested anything. A framed photograph on a table was probably of Pierre's mother.

The white apron appeared at a door nearby and went and said something to Ducos, and he shook his head, and as she was leaving I asked if I could use the bathroom. She showed me, down the hall, and I went, though I really had nothing much to pass but the time, and on the way back there was an open door and I entered. A good detective doesn't have to be invited. There had been no signs anywhere of a daughter, but that room was full of them. It was here. Everything in it said so, and one of the items tagged her good—the contents of a bookcase over by the wall. There were some novels and nonfiction, some of whose titles I recognized, hard covers, and some paperbacks with French titles, but the interesting shelf was the middle one. There were books by Betty Friedan and Kate Millett and four or five more I had heard of, and three by Simone de Beauvoir in French. Of course one or two of them might be on anybody's shelf, but not a whole library. I took one of them out for a look, and her name, Lucile Ducos, was on the title page, and a second one also, and was reaching for another when a voice came from behind.

"What are you doing?"

The white apron. "Nothing much," I said. "I couldn't join in or even understand them and saw these books as I was passing. Are they yours?"

"No. She wouldn't want a man in here, and she wouldn't want a man handling her books." I won't try to spell her accent.

"I'm sorry. Don't tell her, but of course there'll be fingerprints. I didn't touch anything else."

"Did you say your name's Archie Goodwin?"

"I did. It is."

"I knew about you from him. And the radio today. You're a detective. And a policeman wanted to know if you had been here. He told me to call a number if you came."

"I'll bet he did. Are you going to?"

"I don't know, I'll ask Muhsieuw Ducos." I can't spell Muhsieuw the way she said it.

Evidently she wasn't going to leave me there, so I moved, on past her at the door and back to the front room. They were still jabbering, and I went and stood at another window, looking out at the traffic.

It was a quarter past four when we were back in the Heron and rolling out of the parking lot. To Ninth Avenue and downtown. All Wolfe had said was that Ducos had told him something and we would go home and discuss it. He doesn't talk when he's walking or in the car. At the garage Tom said a dick had come a little before noon to see if the car was there—of course it had been—and another one had come around four o'clock and asked if he knew where I had gone with it. From there around the corner and half a block on Thirty-fifth Street to the brownstone, more exercise for Wolfe, and I knew why. If I had driven him home and then taken the car to the garage, somebody might be camped on the stoop.

There wasn't. We mounted the seven steps, and I pushed the button and Fritz came, saw us through the one-way glass panel, slid the chain bolt, and opened the door, and we entered. As I hung Wolfe's coat up he asked Fritz, "Did that man come?"

"Yes, sir. Two of them. They're up there now. Several men came, five of them not counting those two. The phone has rung nine times. Since you weren't sure about dinner, I didn't stuff the capon, so it may be a little late. It's nearly five o'clock."

"It could have been later. Please bring beer. Milk, Archie?"

I said no, make it gin and tonic, and we went to the office. The mail was there under a paperweight on his desk, but after he got his bulk properly distributed in the chair that had been made to order for it, he shoved the mail aside, leaned back, and shut his eyes. I expected, I may even have hoped, to see his lips start moving in and out, but they didn't. He just sat. After four minutes of it, maybe five, I said, "I don't want to interrupt, but you might like to know that the daughter, whose name is Lucile, is a Women's Libber. Not just one of the herd, a real one. She has—"

His eyes had opened. "I was resting. And you know I will not tolerate that locution."

"All right, Liberationist. She has three books by Simone de Beauvoir, who you have admitted can write, in French, and a shelf full of others I have heard of, some of which you have started but didn't finish. Also she wouldn't want a man in her room. I'm talking because someone should say something, and apparently you don't want to."

Fritz came with the tray. There's something I don't like about my taking something from a tray held by Fritz, and as he reached Wolfe's desk I went and got my gin and tonic. Wolfe opened the drawer to get the solid gold opener. When he had poured, he spoke.

"Miss Ducos feeds facts to a computer at New York University. She usually gets home about half past five. You will see her."

"She may not speak to men." I settled back in my chair. He was going to talk.

He grunted. "She will about her father. She was attached to him but didn't want to be. Mr. Ducos is perceptive and articulate

—that is, he was with me. Pierre told you that I am the greatest detective in the world. He told his father that I am the greatest gourmet in the world. His father told me that was why he had told the police nothing, and wouldn't, but he would tell me. He said that only after he learned that I speak French well. Of course that's absurd, but he doesn't know it. Most of what he told me about his son was irrelevant to our purpose, and I won't report it. Or I will, I should, if you insist."

That sounded better than it actually was. Yes, I usually reported in full to him, frequently verbatim, but that wasn't why he was offering to. It was just that if and when he spotted the man who had killed Pierre before I did, he didn't want me to say sure, his father spoke French.

But I kept the grin inside. "Maybe later," I said. "It can wait. Did he tell you anything relevant?"

"He may have. He knew about Pierre's habit of betting on horse races, and they frequently discussed it. He said that Pierre never asked him for money on account of it, but that was a lie. That was one of the few points, very few, about which he was not candid. Also it is one of the points on which you may want a full report later. I mention it now only because it was in a discussion about the betting that Pierre told him about a man giving him a hundred dollars. Last Wednesday morning, six days ago, Pierre told him that one day the preceding week—Mr. Ducos thinks it was Friday but isn't sure—there had been a slip of paper left on a tray with the money by a customer, and later when he went to return it the customer had gone. And the day before, Tuesday—the day before the talk with his father—a man had given him a hundred dollars for the slip of paper."

Wolfe turned a palm up. "That's all. But a hundred dollars for a slip of paper? Even with the soaring inflation, that seems extravagant. And another point. Was the man who gave Pierre that hundred dollars the man who had left the slip of paper on the tray? Of course I tried to get the exact words used by Pierre in the talk with his father, and perhaps I did—the important ones.

Mr. Ducos is certain that he did not use the word *rendre*. Return. Give back. If he had been returning the slip to the man who had left it on the tray, a hundred dollars could have been merely exuberant gratitude, but if it was not the same man—I don't need to descant on that."

I nodded. "A dozen possibles. And if it was the same man, why did Pierre wait four days to return it? Or why didn't he just give it to Felix and ask him to mail it to him? I like it. Is that the crop?"

"Yes. Of course other things that Mr. Ducos told me might possibly repay inquiry, but this was much the most likely." He turned his head to look at the clock. "Nearly two hours to dinner. If you go now?"

"I doubt it. Felix, I suppose, and maybe some of the waiters, but Philip is by far the best bet, and you know how it is in the kitchen at this hour, especially for a sauce man. Also I had four hours' sleep and I'm not—"

The doorbell. I went to the hall for a look, stepped back in, and said, "Cramer."

He made a noise. "How the devil—was he across the street?"

"No, but someone was and phoned. Naturally."

"You'll have to stay."

He rarely uses breath to say things that are obvious, but of course that was. I went and slid the bolt and swung the door open.

Inspector Cramer of Homicide South has been known to call me Archie. He also has been known to pretend he doesn't remember my name, and that time maybe he really didn't. He marched on by, to the office door and in, and when I got there he was saying, ". . . and every goddam minute from the time you woke up until now. You *and* Goodwin. And you'll sign it."

Wolfe was shaking his head, tilted back. "Pfui," he said.

"Don't phooey me! Of all the—"

"*Shut up!*"

Cramer gawked. He had heard Wolfe tell a hundred people to

shut up, and I had heard him tell a thousand, including me, but never Cramer. He didn't believe it.

"I don't invite you to sit," Wolfe said, "or to remove your coat and hat, because I am going to tell you nothing. No, I retract that. I do tell you that I know nothing about the death of Pierre Ducos except what Mr. Goodwin has told me, and he has told Mr. Stebbins everything he told me. Beyond that I shall tell you absolutely nothing. Of course I had to permit examination of that room by qualified men, and I left instructions to admit them. They are still up there. If we are taken in custody as material witnesses, by either you or the District Attorney, we'll stand mute. Released on bail, we'll still stand mute. I am going to learn who killed that man in my house. I doubt if you can and I hope you don't, except from me when I'm ready to tell you."

Wolfe aimed a straight finger at him, up at his face, another first. "If I sound uncivil, I do not apologize. I am in a rage and out of control. Whether you have warrants or not, arrest us now and take us; let's get that over with. I have a job to do." He extended his arms, stretched out, the wrists together for handcuffs. Beautiful. I would have loved to do it too, but that would have been piling it on.

If Cramer had had cuffs in his pocket he might actually have used them, judging from the look on his big red face. Knowing Wolfe as well as he did, what *could* he do? His mouth opened and closed again. He looked at me and back at Wolfe. "Out of control," he growled. "Balls. *You* out of control. I know one thing. I know—"

"Oh! We didn't know you were here, Inspector."

Two men were there at the door, a tall rangy one and a broad bulky one with only one arm. Of course I should have heard them; my ears must have been more eager to hear what Cramer would say than I realized. When he turned to face them they saluted, but he didn't return it.

"It took you long enough," he said.

"Yes, sir. It was a job. We didn't know you were here. We—"

"I came to see why it took so damn long. Did you— No. You can tell me in the car." He was moving. They sidestepped to let him by and followed him out. I stayed put. Experts wouldn't need help opening a door. When the sound came of the front door opening and closing, I went for a look down the hall, came back, and said, "What a break for him. He *couldn't* have left without us. He ought to move them up a peg. Of course it was a break for us too, with you out of control."

"Grrrh," he said. "Sit down."

4

AT TEN O'CLOCK that evening I was standing by a reading lamp, flipping through the pages of a book entitled *Les Sauces du Monde*. Going through a room trying to find something doesn't take long if you're after a diamond necklace or an elephant tusk or a gun. But if it's a twenty-dollar bill, anything at all that could be between the pages of a book without bulging it, that takes time if there are books in the room. For the Library of Congress, I would say 2748 years.

Most of the forty-some books on shelves in Pierre Ducos's room were about cooking. What I was after didn't have to be a piece of paper, but that was the most likely, since I wanted something, anything, that could lead to either the man who had left the slip of paper on the tray or the one who had paid a C for it. One item that had seemed possible was a notebook I found in a drawer that had lists of names on several pages, but Lucile Ducos had told me they were the names of men who gave big tips. She said Pierre hadn't been good at remembering names and he had written them down for twenty years.

I hadn't been in her room. When, arriving, I had told her grandfather, with her as interpreter, that I wanted to take a look in Pierre's room, and why, I had got the impression that she didn't like it, but he had got emphatic and it took. I had also got the impression that she was staying with me to see if I took anything and if so what. Getting impressions from her wasn't difficult, beginning with the impression that it didn't matter whether I had two legs or four legs, or whether I wore my face in front or behind. But *she* mattered—I mean to her. Her face, which wasn't bad at all, was well cared for, also her nice brown hair, and the cut and hang of her light-brown dress were just right. It was hard to believe she went to all that trouble just for the mirror.

She was seated in an easy chair the other side of the reading lamp. When I did the last book and put it back on the shelf, I turned to her and said, "I suppose you're right, if he put something somewhere it would be in this room. Have you remembered anything he said?"

"No."

"Have you tried to?"

"I told you I knew I couldn't because he hadn't said anything."

Her voice had a little too much nose. I looked down at her. Up to a few inches above her knees, she had good legs. A pity. I decided to try another approach. "You know, Miss Ducos," I said, "I have tried to be polite and sympathetic, I really have. But I wonder why you don't give a damn who killed your father. That doesn't seem very—well, natural."

She nodded. "You would. You think I should be weeping and wailing or maybe doing a Medea. Bullshit. I was a good daughter, good enough. Of course I give a damn who killed him, but I don't think you're going to find out the way you're going at it, all this about a man who gave him some money for a piece of paper. Or if you do, it won't be by nagging me to remember something that didn't happen."

"What would you suggest? How would you do it?"

"I don't know. I'm not a great detective like Nero Wolfe. But you say what killed him was a bomb put in his pocket by someone. Who put it there? I'd find out where he was yesterday and who he saw. That would be the first thing I would do."

I nodded. "Sure. And have your toes tramped on by a few dozen homicide experts who are doing just that. If he can be tagged that way, they'll get him without any help from Nero Wolfe. Of course one person your father saw yesterday was you. I haven't asked you about your relations with him, and I'm not going to, because the cops certainly have. And they're asking around about you. You were at the District Attorney's office five hours, you said, so you know how that is. They know all about people killing their fathers. Also, of course they asked you if there was anyone who might have wanted him dead. What did you say?"

"I said no."

"But someone did want him dead."

She sneered. I admit I didn't like her, but I'm not being unfair. She sneered. "I knew you'd say that," she said. "They did too, and it's not only obvious, it's dumb. Somebody might have thought his coat belonged to someone else."

"Then you think it was just a mistake?"

"I didn't say I *think* it. I said it might have been."

"Didn't your grandfather tell you what Nero Wolfe told him your father told me?"

"No. He never tells me anything. He thinks women haven't any brains. You probably do too."

I wanted to say that I merely thought *some* women were a little shy on brains, present company not excepted, but I skipped it. I said, "Your father told me that a man was going to kill him, so it wasn't a mistake. Also it wasn't you, since you're not a man. So let's go back. Evidently your father didn't agree with your grandfather about women, because your grandfather told Mr. Wolfe that your father often asked your advice about things. That's why I think he might have told you something about a man who gave him a hundred dollars for a slip of paper."

"He never asked my *advice*. He just wanted to see what I would say."

I gave up. I wanted to ask her what the difference was between asking her advice and wanting to see what she would say, just to see what she would say, but we were expecting company at the office at eleven o'clock or soon after and I should be there. So I gave up on her, and I had finished the job on the room, since it wasn't likely that he had pried up a floorboard or taken the back off a picture frame. I will concede that she had fairly good manners. She went to the hall with me and opened the door and told me good night. Apparently Mr. Ducos and the white apron had both gone to bed.

It was ten after eleven when I mounted the stoop of the old brownstone, found the bolt wasn't on so I didn't need help to get in, and went to the office. Wolfe would be deep in either a book or a crossword puzzle, but he wasn't. In one of my desk drawers I keep street maps of all five New York boroughs, and he had them, with Manhattan spread out covering his desk blotter and then some. To my knowledge it was the first time he had ever given it a look. It might be supposed that I wondered what he was after, but I didn't because I had learned long ago that wondering what a genius was after was a waste of time. If it really meant anything, which I doubted, he would tell me when he felt like it. As I swiveled my chair and sat to face him, he started folding it up, his fingers quick and nimble and precise, as they always were. Of course they had a lot of practice up in the plant rooms, from nine to eleven mornings and four to six afternoons, but that day he hadn't been there at all.

As he folded he spoke. "I was calculating distances—the restaurant, and Pierre's home, and here. He arrived here at ten minutes to one. Where had he been? Where had his coat been?"

"I'll have to apologize," I said, "to his daughter. I told her that if that kind of detecting will do it they won't need your help. Does it look that bad?"

"No. As you know, I prefer not to read when I may be interrupted at any moment. What did she tell you?"

"Nothing. It's possible she has nothing to tell, but I don't believe it. She sat for an hour with her eye on me while I went over Pierre's room, to make sure I didn't pinch a pair of socks. She's an anomaly—I *think* that's the word I want. Or make—"

"It isn't. A person can't be an anomaly."

"All right, she's a phony. A woman who has those books with her name in them wants men to stop making women sex symbols, and if she really wants them to stop she wouldn't keep her skin like that, and her hair, and blow her hard-earned pay on a dress that sets her off. Of course she can't help her legs. She's a phony. Since Pierre said it was a man, I admit she probably didn't put the bomb in his pocket, but I would buy it that he told her about the slip of paper and showed it to her, and she knows who killed him and is going to put the squeeze on him, or try to. And she'll get killed and we'll have that too. I suggest that we put a tail on her. If you have other plans for me, get Fred or Orrie, or maybe even Saul. Do you want it verbatim?"

"Do I need it?"

"No."

"Then just the substance."

I crossed my legs. "First she interpreted for me with her grandfather while I asked for permission to take a look at Pierre's room, and the other points you wanted covered. Of course she could have hashed that—with an interpreter you never know for sure. Then she went with me—"

The doorbell rang, and I got up and went. We had expected Philip around eleven and Felix a little later, but they were both there. And from the look on their faces, they weren't speaking. They spoke to me as I let them in and took their coats, but apparently not to each other. In the office, when they were seated after being greeted by Wolfe's most exaggerated nod, a full half-inch—of course Felix in the red leather chair near the end of Wolfe's desk—Philip sat stiff with no mouth showing on his dark-skinned square face because his lips were pressed so tight, and Felix didn't really sit, he just got his rump on the edge of the chair and blurted, "I kept Philip there, Mr. Wolfe, because he lied to me. As you know, I—"

"If you please." Of course Felix had often heard that tone when Wolfe had been his boss as trustee. "You're upset. I suppose you've had a hard day, but so have I. I'll have beer. Brandy for you?"

"No, sir. Nothing."

"Philip?"

Philip shook his head. I detoured around him on my way to the kitchen. When I came back, Felix was sitting, not perching, and was talking: ". . . eight of them. They kept coming and going all afternoon and evening. I got their names. It was the worst day we have ever had since the day Mr. Vukcic died. The first two came just at the end of lunch, three o'clock, and it never stopped, right on through dinner. It was terrible. Everybody, even the dishwasher. The main thing with them was the dump room—you know, Mr. Vukcic called it that, so we do—the room in the back where the men leave their things. They took everybody there, one at a time, and asked about Pierre's coat. What is it about Pierre's coat?"

"You'll have to ask them." The foam in the glass had reached the right level, and Wolfe picked it up and drank. "You have me to thank for the day they gave you. Because he was killed here, in my house. But for that it would be mere routine for them. Did they arrest anyone?"

"No, sir. I thought one of them was going to arrest me. He said he knew there was something special between you and Pierre, and Mr. Goodwin too, and he said I must know about it. He told me to get my coat and hat, but then he changed his mind. He was the same with—"

"His name was Rowcliff."

"Yes, sir." Felix nodded. "It may be true that you know everything. Mr. Vukcic told me that you thought you did. That man was the same with Philip because I told him that he was Pierre's best friend." He looked at Philip, not as a friend, and went back to Wolfe. "Philip may have lied to him, I don't know, I know he lied to me. You remember what Mr. Vukcic told Noel that time when he fired him. He told him it wasn't because he stole a goose, anyone might steal a goose, it was because he lied about it. He said he could keep it a good restaurant even if some of them stole things sometimes, but not if anybody lied to him, because he had to know what happened. I always remember that and I will not permit them to lie to me, and they know it. If I don't know what happened, it won't be a good restaurant. So when the last one left, I took Philip upstairs and told him I had to know everything about Pierre that he knew, and he lied. I have learned to tell when one of them is lying. I'm not as good at it as Mr. Vukcic was, but I can nearly always tell. Look at him."

We looked. Philip looked back at Felix and unglued his mouth to say, "I told you I was lying. I admitted it."

"You did not. That's another lie."

Philip looked at Wolfe. "I told him I was leaving something out because I couldn't remember. Isn't that admitting it, Mr. Wolfe?"

"It's a nice point," Wolfe said. "It deserves discussion, but I think not here and now. You were leaving out something that Pierre had done or said?"

"Yes, sir. I admitted I couldn't remember it."

Wolfe grunted. "This afternoon I asked you to try to recall everything he said yesterday, and you said you would but you couldn't do it at the restaurant. Now you admit there was something you can't remember?"

"It wasn't that, Mr. Wolfe. It wasn't what he said yesterday."

"Nonsense. A rigmarole. You're wriggling. Do you want me to form the conjecture that you killed him? Do you or don't you want the murderer exposed and punished? Do you or don't you know something that might help to identify him? You said you wept when you learned he was dead. Did you indeed?"

Philip's mouth was closed, clamped again. His eyes closed. He shook his head several times, slow. He opened his eyes, turned his head to look at Felix, turned it back and on around to look at me, and back again to Wolfe, and spoke. "I want to talk to you alone, Mr. Wolfe."

Wolfe turned to Felix. "The front room, Felix. As you know, it's soundproofed."

"But I want—"

"Confound it, it's past midnight. I'll tell you later, or I won't. Certainly *he* won't. I'm spent, and so are you."

I got up and crossed to open the door to the front room, and Felix came. I stuck my head in to see that the door to the hall was closed, shut that one, and returned to my desk. As I sat, Philip said, "I said alone, Mr. Wolfe. Just you."

"No. If Mr. Goodwin leaves and you tell me anything that suggests action, I'll have the bother of repeating to him."

"Then I must—you must both promise not to tell Felix. Pierre was a proud man, Mr. Wolfe, I told you that. He was proud of his work and he didn't want to be just a good waiter, he wanted to be the *best* waiter. He wanted Mr. Vukcic to think he was the best waiter in the best restaurant in the world, and then he wanted Felix to think that. Maybe he does think that, and that's why you must promise not to tell him. He must not know that Pierre did something that no good waiter would ever do."

"We can't promise not to tell him. We can only promise not to tell him unless we must, unless it becomes impossible to find the murderer and expose him without telling Felix. I can promise that, and do. Archie?"

"Yes, sir," I said firmly. "I promise that. Cross my heart and hope to die. That's American, Philip, you may not know it. It means I would rather die than tell him."

"You have already told us," Wolfe said, "that he told you about getting orders mixed and serving them wrong, so that can't be it."

"No, sir. That was just yesterday. It was something much worse. Something he told me last week, Monday, a week ago yesterday. He told me a man had left a piece of paper on the tray with the money, and he had kept it, a piece of paper with something written on it. He told me he had kept it because the man had gone when he went to return it, and then he didn't give it to Felix to send it to him because what was written on it was a man's name and address and he knew the name and he wondered about it. He said he still had it, the piece of paper. So after you talked to me today, after you told me he said a man was going to kill him, I wondered if it could have been on account of that. I thought it might even have been the man whose name was on the paper. I knew it couldn't have been the man who had left the paper on the tray, because he was dead."

"Dead?"

"Yes, sir."

"How did you know he was dead?"

"It had been on the radio and in the paper. Pierre had told me it was Mr. Bassett who left the paper on the tray. We all knew about Mr. Bassett because he always paid in cash and he was a big tipper. Very big. Once he gave Felix a five-hundred-dollar bill."

I suppose I must have heard that, since I just wrote it, but if I was listening it was only with one ear. Millions of people knew about Harvey H. Bassett, president of NATELEC, National Electronics Industries, not because he was a big tipper but because he had been murdered just four days ago, last Friday night.

Wolfe hadn't batted an eye, but he cleared his throat and swallowed. "Yes," he said, "it certainly couldn't have been Mr. Bassett. But the man whose name was on the slip of paper—what *was* his name? Of course Pierre showed it to you."

"No, sir, he didn't."

"At least he told you, he must have. You said he knew the name and wondered about it. So unquestionably he told you what it was. And you will tell me."

"No, sir, I can't. I don't know."

Wolfe's head turned to me. "Go and tell Felix he may as well leave. Tell him we may be engaged with Philip all night."

I left my chair, but so did Philip. "No, you won't," he said, and he meant it. "I'm going home. This has been the worst day of my whole life, and I'm fifty-four years old. First Pierre dead, and then all day knowing I ought to tell this, first Felix and then you and then the police, and wondering if Archie Goodwin killed him. Now I'm thinking maybe I shouldn't have told you, maybe I should have told the police, but then I think how you were with Mr. Vukcic and when he died. And I know how he was about you. But I've told you everything—*everything*. I can't tell you any more." He headed for the door.

I looked at Wolfe, but he shook his head, so I merely went to the hall and the front, no hurry. Probably Philip wouldn't let me help him on with his coat—but he did. No good nights. I opened the door, closed it after him, returned to the office, and asked Wolfe, "Do you want Felix?"

"No." He was on his feet. "Of course he can tell us about Bassett, but I'm played out, and so are you. One question: Does Philip know the name on that paper?"

"One will get you ten, no. He told me to my face that I may be a murderer and called me Archie Goodwin. He was unloading."

"Confound it. Tell Felix he'll hear from me tomorrow. Today. Good night." He moved.

5

THE DINNER paid for by Harvey H. Bassett in an upstairs room at Rusterman's Friday evening, October 18, had been stag. The guests:

Albert O. Judd, lawyer
Francis Ackerman, lawyer
Roman Vilar, Vilar Associates, industrial security
Ernest Urquhart, lobbyist
Willard K. Hahn, banker
Benjamin Igoe, electronics engineer

Putting that here, I'm way ahead of myself and of you, but I don't like making lists and I wanted to get it down. Also, when I typed it that Wednesday to put on Wolfe's desk, I looked it over to decide if one of them was a murderer and if so which one, and you may want to play that game too. Not that it had to be one of them. The fact that they had been present when Bassett left the slip of paper among the bills on the tray didn't make them any better candidates than anyone else for who could have been with him in a stolen automobile on West Ninety-third Street around midnight a week later with a gun in his hand, but we had to start somewhere, and at least they had known him. Possibly one of them had given him the slip of paper.

I got to bed Tuesday night at twenty past one, almost exactly twenty-four hours after the bomb had interrupted me before I got my pants off. It was a good bet that I would be interrupted before I got them on again Wednesday morning by an invitation from the DA's office, but I wasn't, so I got my full eight hours, and I needed them, and it was ten minutes to ten when I entered the kitchen, went to the refrigerator for orange juice, told Fritz good morning, and asked if Wolfe had had breakfast, and Fritz said yes, at a quarter past eight as usual.

"Was he dressed?"

"Of course."

"*Not* of course. He was played out, he said so himself. He went up?"

"Of course."

"All right, have it your way. Any word for me?"

"No. I'm played out too, Archie, all day the phone ringing and people coming, and I didn't know where he was."

I went to the little table and sat and reached to the rack for the *Times*. It had made the front page, a two-column lead toward the bottom and continued on page 19, where there were pictures of both of us. Of course I was honored because I had found the body. Also of course I read every word, some of it twice, but none of it was news to me, and my mind kept sliding off. Why the hell hadn't he told Fritz to send me up? I was on my third sausage and second buckwheat cake when the phone rang, and I scowled at it as I reached. Again of course, the DA.

But it wasn't; it was Lon Cohen of the *Gazette*.

"Nero Wolfe's office, Arch—"

"Where in God's name were you all day yesterday, and why aren't you in jail?"

"Look, Lon, I—"

"Will you come here, or must I go there?"

"Right now, neither one, and quit interrupting. I admit I could tell you twenty-seven things that your readers have a right to know, but this is a free country and I want to stay free. The minute I can spill one bean I know where to find you. I'm expecting a call so I'm hanging up." I hung up.

I will never know whether there was something wrong with

the buckwheat cakes or with me. If it was the cakes, Fritz *was* played out. I made myself eat the usual four to keep him from asking questions and finding out that he had left something out or put too much of something in.

In the office I pretended it was just another day—dusting, emptying the wastebaskets, changing the water in the vase, opening the mail, and so forth. Then I went to the shelf where we keep the *Times* and the *Gazette* for two weeks, got them for the last four days, and took them to my desk. Of course I had read the accounts of the murder of Harvey H. Bassett, but now it was more than just news. The body had been found in a parked Dodge Coronet on West Ninety-third Street near Riverside Drive late Friday night by a cop on his rounds. Only one bullet, a .38, which had entered at exactly the right spot to go through his pump and keep going, clear through. It had been found stuck in the right front door, so the trigger had been pulled by the driver of the car, unless Bassett had pulled it himself, but by Monday's *Times* that was out. It was murder.

I was on Tuesday's *Gazette* when the sound came of the elevator descending. My watch said 11:01. Right on schedule. I swiveled and as Wolfe entered said brightly, "Good morning. I'm having a look at the reports on Harvey H. Bassett. If you're interested, I'm through with the *Times*."

He put a raceme of orchids which I didn't bother to identify in the vase on his desk, and sat. "You're spleeny. You shouldn't be. After that night and yesterday, you might sleep until noon, and there was no urgency. As for Mr. Bassett, I keep my copies of the *Times* in my room for a month, as you know, and I took—"

The doorbell. I went to the hall for a look and stepped back in. "I don't think you've ever met him. Assistant District Attorney Coggin. Daniel F. Coggin. Friendly type with a knife up his sleeve. Handshaker."

"Bring him," he said, and reached for the pile of mail.

So when I ushered the member of the bar in after giving him as good a hand as he gave and taking his coat and hat, Wolfe had a circular in one hand and an unfolded letter in the other, and it wouldn't have been polite to put him to the trouble of putting one of them down, so Coggin didn't. Evidently, though he hadn't met him, he knew about his kinks. He just said heartily, "I don't think I've ever had the pleasure of meeting you, Mr. Wolfe, so I welcome this opportunity." He sat, in the red leather chair, and sent his eyes around. "Nice room. A *good* room. That's a beautiful rug."

"A gift from the Shah of Iran," Wolfe said.

Coggin must have known it was a barefaced lie, but he said, "I wish he'd give me one. Beautiful." He glanced at his wristwatch. "You're a busy man, and I'll be as brief as possible. The District Attorney is wondering why you and Mr. Goodwin were—well, couldn't be found yesterday, though that isn't how he put it— when you knew you were wanted and needed. And your telephone wasn't answered. Nor your doorbell."

"We had errands to do and did them. No one was here but Mr. Brenner, my cook, and when we are out he prefers not to answer bells."

Coggin smiled. *"He* prefers?"

Wolfe smiled back, but his smile shows only at one corner of his mouth, and it takes good eyes to see it. "Good cooks must be humored, Mr. Coggin."

"I wouldn't know, Mr. Wolfe. I haven't got a cook, can't afford it. Now. If you're wondering why I came instead of sending for you, we discussed it at the office. What you said to Inspector Cramer yesterday. Considering your record and your customary—uh—reactions. It was decided to have your license as a private investigator revoked at once, but I thought that was too drastic and suggested that upon reflection you might have realized that you had been—uh—impetuous. I have in my pocket warrants for your arrest, you and Mr. Goodwin, as material witnesses, but I don't *want* to serve them. I would rather not. I even came alone, I insisted on that. I can understand, I *do* understand, why you reacted as you did to Inspector Cramer, but you and Goodwin can't withhold information regarding the murder of a man in your house—a man you had known for years and had talked with many times. I don't *want* you and Goodwin to lose your licenses. He can take shorthand and he can type. I want to leave here with signed statements."

When Wolfe is facing the red leather chair he has to turn his head a quarter-circle to face me. He turned. "Your notebook, Archie."

I opened a drawer and got it, and a pen. He leaned back, closed his eyes, and spoke.

"When Pierre Ducos died by violence in a room of my house at— The exact time, Archie?"

"One-twenty-four."

"One-twenty-four a.m. on October twenty-ninth, comma, nineteen seventy-four, comma, I knew nothing about him or any of his affairs except that he was an experienced and competent restaurant waiter. Period. Archie Goodwin also knew only that about him, comma, plus what he had learned in a brief conversation with him when he arrived at my house shortly before he died. Period. All of that conversation was given verbatim by Mr. Goodwin in a signed statement given by him to a police officer that night at my house. Period. Therefore all knowledge that could possibly be relevant to the death by violence of Pierre Ducos known to either Mr. Goodwin or me at the moment his body was discovered by Mr. Goodwin has been given to the police. Paragraph.

"Since that moment—dash—the moment that the body was discovered—dash—Mr. Goodwin and I have made various inquiries of various persons for the purpose of learning who was responsible for the death of Pierre Ducos in my house, comma, and we are going to continue such inquiries. Period. We have made them and shall make them not as licensed private investigators, comma, but as private citizens on whose private premises a capital crime has been committed. Period. We believe our right to make such an inquiry cannot be successfully challenged, comma, and if such a challenge is made we will resist it. Period. That right would not be affected by revocation of our licenses as investigators. Paragraph.

"Information obtained by us during our inquiry may be divulged by us, comma, or it may not, comma, either to the police or to the public. Period. The decision regarding disclosure will be solely at our discretion and will. Period. If the issue is raised of our responsibilities as private citizens it will of course be decided by the proper legal procedures. Period. If our licenses have not been revoked our responsibilities as private investigators will not be involved. Period. If they have been revoked those responsibilities will not exist. Paragraph.

"We will continue to cooperate with the police to the extent required by law—dash—for instance, comma, we will permit entry at any reasonable time to the room where the crime occurred. Period. We approve and applaud a vigorous effort by the police to find the culprit and will continue to do so. Period."

He opened his eyes and straightened up. "On my letterhead, single-spaced, wide margins, four carbons. All to be signed by me, and by you if you wish. Give the original to Mr. Coggin. Mail one carbon to Mr. Cramer. Take one to Mr. Cohen and offer it as an item for publication in the *Gazette* tomorrow. If he rejects it, make it a two-column display advertisement in ten-point. Take one to the *Times* and offer it, not as an advertisement. If Mr. Coggin interferes by serving his warrants and arresting us before you get it typed, on being taken into custody I will exercise my right to telephone a lawyer, dictate it to Mr. Parker's secretary, and tell him what to do."

He turned his head the quarter-circle. "If you wish to comment, Mr. Coggin, you'll have to raise your voice. Mr. Goodwin will not use a noiseless typewriter."

Coggin was smiling. "It's not up to your usual standard. A lousy cheap bluff."

"Then call it. I believe that's the idiom for the proper reaction to a cheap bluff." Wolfe turned a palm up. "Surely it's obvious; it

was to Mr. Cramer. I do approve and applaud the effort by the
police to do their duty under law, but in this case I hope they fail.
I invite you to have a look at the room upstairs directly over my
bedroom. A man was killed in it as I lay asleep. I intend to find
the man who did it and bring him to account, with the help of
Mr. Goodwin, whose self-esteem is as wounded as my own. He
took him to that room."

His fingers curled into the palm. "No. Not a bluff. I doubt if I
am taking a serious risk, but if so, then I am. The constant petty
behests of life permit few opportunities for major satisfactions,
and when one is offered it should be seized. You know what I
told Mr. Cramer we will do if we are charged and taken, so there
is no need to repeat it." His head turned. "Type it, Archie."

I swiveled and swung the machine around and got paper and
carbons. Much of the room shows in the six-by-four mirror on
the wall back of my desk, so I knew I wasn't missing anything
while I hit the keys, because Coggin's mouth stayed shut. His
eyes were aimed in my direction. The amount of copy was just
right, wide-margined, for a nice neat page. I rolled it out,
removed the carbon paper, and took it to Wolfe, and he signed
all of them, including the one we would keep, and I signed under
him without bothering to sit.

And when I handed the original to Coggin he said, "I'll take
the carbons too. All of them."

"Sorry," I said, "I only work here and I like the job, so I
follow instructions."

"Give them to him," Wolfe said. "You have the notebook."

I handed them over. He put the original with them, jiggled
them on the little stand to even the edges, folded them, and stuck
them in his inside breast pocket. He smiled at Wolfe. Of course
the typing and signing had given him seven minutes to look at all
angles. "Probably," he said, "you could name him right now and
you only have to collect the pieces." He palmed the chair arms
for leverage and got to his feet. "I hope there'll be other warrants, not for material witnesses, and I hope I have it and you get

ten years with no parole." He turned and stepped, but halfway to the door he stopped and turned to say over his shoulder, "Don't come, Goodwin. You smell."

When the sound came of the front door closing, I crossed over for a look. He was out. I crossed back and said, "So you didn't give me an errand because you knew one of them would come. Wonderful."

He grunted. "I have told you a dozen times, sarcasm is the most futile of weapons. It doesn't cut, it merely bounces off. Why did he want the carbons?"

"Souvenirs. Autographs. Signed by both of us. Someday they'll be auctioned off at Sotheby's." I looked at my watch. "It's twenty minutes to noon. Things will be all set for lunch and the customers won't start coming until nearly one. Or have you a better place to start than Felix?"

"You know I haven't. We want everything he knows about Mr. Bassett and his guests that evening. Unless—you have slept on it, so I ask again, does Philip know what was on that slip of paper?"

"It's still no. As I said, he was unloading. He thinks the name on it might have been Archie Goodwin. Pierre told him he wondered about it. All right, I probably won't be here for lunch."

"A moment. One detail. If Felix supplies names, even one, and you get to him, it might serve to tell him that Pierre told you that he saw one of them hand Mr. Bassett a slip of paper. It *might*. Consider it."

"Yeah. And Pierre's dead."

I went to the hall and to the rack for my coat. No hat. The thermometer outside said 38, more like December than October, no sun, but I have rules too. No hat before Thanksgiving. Rain or snow is good for hair.

6

WITH FELIX it was all negatives, and negatives are no good either to write or to read. Except for preferences and opinions about food and how it should be served, I knew more about Harvey H. Bassett than he did, since I had read the newspapers twice and he may not have read them at all. Television and radio, and his working day was a good twelve hours. On the big question, the names of the guests at the dinner on October 18, nearly two weeks ago, he was a complete blank. He had never seen any of them before or since. All he knew was that it had been stag. Evidently he thought better of me than Philip did; he said he had some fresh pompano up from the Gulf and wanted to feed me, but I declined with thanks.

It was 12:42 when I left by the front door and headed uptown. One of my more useless habits is timing all walks, though it may be helpful only about one time in a hundred. It took nine minutes to the *Gazette* building. Lon Cohen's room, two doors down the hall from the publisher's on the twentieth floor, barely had enough space for a big desk with three phones on it, one chair besides his, and shelves with a few books and a thousand newspapers. It was his lunch hour, so I expected to find him alone, and he was.

"I'll be damned," he said. "You still loose?"

"No." I sat. "I'm a fugitive. I came to bring you a new picture of me. The one you ran Sunday, my nose is crooked. I admit it's no treat, but it's not crooked."

"It should be, after Monday night. Damn it, Archie, I'm an hour behind. I'll get Landry, there's a room down the hall, and—"

"No. Not even what I had for breakfast. As I said on the phone, when I can spill one bean you'll get it." I rose. "Right now we could use a fact or two, but if you're an hour behind—" I was going.

"Sit down. All right, I'll be two hours behind. But I'm not going to starve." He took a healthy bite of a tuna-and-lettuce sandwich on whole wheat.

"Not an hour." I sat. "Maybe only three minutes if you can tell me the names of six men who ate dinner on Harvey H. Bassett at Rusterman's, Friday, October eighteenth."

"What?" He stopped chewing to stare. "Bassett? What has that got to do with a bomb killing a man in Nero Wolfe's house?"

"It's connected, but that's off the record. Right now everything's off the record. Repeat, *everything*. Pierre Ducos was the waiter at that dinner. Do you know who was there?"

"No. I didn't know *he* was there."

"How soon can you find out and keep me out of it?"

"Maybe a day, maybe a week. It might be an hour if we could get to Doh Ray Me."

"Who is Doh Ray Me?"

"His wife. Widow. Of course you don't call her that now, not to her face. She's holed up. She won't see anybody, not even the DA. Her doctor eats and sleeps there. They say. What are you staring for? Is *my* nose crooked?"

"I'll be damned." I stood up. "Of course. Why the hell didn't I remember? I must be in shock. See you tomorrow night—I hope. Forget I was here." I went.

There was no phone booth on that floor, so I went to the elevator. On the way down I pinched my memory. Having met only about a tenth of the characters—poets from Bolivia, pianists from Hungary, girls from Wyoming or Utah—who had been given a hand by Lily Rowan, I had never seen Dora Miller. Arriving in

New York from Kansas, she had been advised by an artist's agent to change her name to Doremi, and when nobody had pronounced it right, had changed it again to Doraymee. You would think that a singer with that name would surely go far, but at the time Lily had told me about her she had been doing TV commercials. Though the *Times* may not have mentioned that Mrs. Harvey H. Bassett had once been Doraymee, the *Gazette* must have, and I missed it. Shock.

I entered one of the ten booths on the ground floor, shut the door, and dialed a number, and after eight rings, par for that number, a voice came. "Hello?" She always makes it a question.

"Hello. The top of the afternoon to you."

"Well. I haven't rung your number even once, so you owe me a pat on the head or a pat where you think it would do the most good. Are you alive and well? Are you at home?"

"I'm alive. I'm also ten short blocks from you. Only a ten-minute walk if you feel like company."

"You are not company. As you know, we are still trying to decide what each other is. I speak English. Lunch is nearly ready. Cross on the green."

We hung up. That's one of the many good points: *we* hung up.

Even with another tenant, it would be a pleasure to enter that penthouse on East Sixty-third Street, but of course with another tenant it wouldn't be furnished like that. The only two things that I definitely would scrap are the painting on the living-room wall by de Kooning and the electric fireplace in the spare bedroom. I also like the manners. Lily nearly always opens the door herself, and she doesn't lift a hand when a man takes his coat off in the vestibule. We usually don't kiss for a greeting, but that time she put her hands on my arms and offered, and I accepted. More, I returned the compliment.

She backed up and demanded, "Where were you and what were you doing at half past one Monday night, October twenty-eighth?"

"Try again," I said. "You fumbled it. Tuesday morning, October twenty-ninth. But first I want to confess. I'm here under false pretenses. I came because I need help."

She nodded. "Certainly. I knew that when you said the top of the afternoon to me. You only remind me that I'm Irish when you want something. So you're in a hurry and we'll go straight to the table. There's enough." She led the way through the living room to the den, where the desk and files and shelves and typewriter stand barely leave room enough for a table that two can eat on. As we sat, Mimi came with a loaded tray.

"Go ahead," Lily said.

I want to like my manners too, so I waited until Mimi had finished serving and gone and we had taken bites of celery. Also, at Lily's table, especially when no guest had been expected, often not even Fritz would have known what was on his plate just by looking at it, so I looked at her with my eyebrows up.

She nodded. "You've never had it. We're trying it and haven't decided. Mushrooms and soybeans and black walnuts and sour cream. Don't tell *him*. If you can't get it down, Mimi will do a quick omelet. Even he admitted she could do an omelet. At the ranch."

I had taken a forkload. It didn't need much chewing, not even the walnuts, because they had been pulverized or something. When it was down I said, "I want to make it perfectly clear that—"

"Don't *do* that! I've told you. Even a joke about him turns my stomach."

"You're too careless with pronouns. Your hims. Your first him's opinion of your second him is about the same as yours. So is mine. As for this mix, I'm like you, I haven't decided. I admit it's different." I loaded a fork.

"I'll just watch your face. Tell me why you came."

I waited until the second forkful was with the first. "As I said, I need help. You once told me about a girl from Kansas named Doraymee. Remember?"

"Of course I do. I saw her yesterday."

"You *saw* her? *Yesterday?* You saw Mrs. Harvey H. Bassett?"

"Yes. You must know about her husband, since you always read about murders. She phoned me yesterday afternoon and said she was—" She stopped with her mouth half open. "What is this? She asked about you, and now you're asking about her. What's going on?"

My mouth was half open too. "I don't believe it. Are you saying that Mrs. Bassett phoned you to ask about me? I don't—"

"I didn't say that. She phoned to ask me to come and hold her hand—that was what she wanted, but she didn't say so. She said she just had to see me, I suppose because of what I had done before, when she couldn't make it in New York and was going back home to get a meal. I hadn't really done much, just paid for her room and board for a year. I hadn't seen her for—oh, three or four years. I went, and we talked for an hour or more, and she asked if I had seen you since her husband died. I thought she was just talking. Also she said she had read some of your books about Nero Wolfe's cases, and that surprised me because I knew she never read books. I thought she was just talking to get her mind off of her troubles, but now *you* ask about *her*. So I want to know—" She bit it off and stared at me. "My god, Escamillo, is it possible that I *am* capable of jealousy? Of course, if I could be about anybody, it would be about you, but I have always thought . . . I refuse to believe it."

"Relax." I reached to draw fingertips across the back of her hand. "Probably you have been jealous about me since the day you first caught sight of me and heard my voice, that's only natural, but Doraymee has never seen me and I have never seen her. Our asking about each other is just a coincidence. Usually I'm suspicious of coincidences, but I love this one. I now tell you something that is absolutely not for publication. Not yet. There's a connection between the two murders—Bassett and Pierre Ducos—and it's possible that Doraymee knows something that will help. A week before he was killed—Friday evening, October eighteenth—Bassett treated six men to a meal at Rusterman's, and Nero Wolfe wants to know the names of the six men, and so do I. Possibly she knows. The name of even one would help. Lon Cohen of the *Gazette,* whom you have met, says that she has holed up and won't see anybody. I'm not particular; either you might call her and ask her to see me, or you might go and ask her for the names, or you might just ask for them on the phone. As I said, even one of them. That's what I came for, and I want to thank you for this delicious hash. I also want the recipe for Fritz." I loaded my fork.

She took a bite of celery and chewed. That's another good point: her face is just as attractive when she is chewing celery or even a good big bite of steak. She swallowed. "This is the third time you've asked me to help," she said. "I didn't mind the other two. In fact I enjoyed it."

I nodded. "And there's no reason not to enjoy this one. I wouldn't ask you to snoop on a friend, you know that. I assume—we assume—that she would like to have the man who killed her husband tagged and nailed. So would we. I admit the one we have *got* to tag is the one who killed Pierre Ducos there in that house when I was going to bed just thirty feet away, but as I said, they're connected. I can't guarantee she will never be sorry she told you these names; when you're investigating a murder you can't guarantee anything, but you can name the odds. A thousand to one." I loaded my fork. I *think* that stuff was edible; my mind wasn't on it.

"I'd rather just phone and ask her. What if she says she doesn't know their names and I think she's lying? I like her, you can't help but like her, but she's a pretty good liar. I don't want to needle her now. She's low, *very* low."

"Of course not. Make it simple. Leave me out. Just say somebody told you she saw Bassett at Rusterman's with five or six men just a week before he was killed and they didn't look very jolly and she wondered if one of them killed him. Nuts. Listen to me. Telling *you* how to use your tongue."

"No butter today, thank you. All right. There's lemon-sherry pudding and I want to enjoy it, so I'll go to the bedroom and get it done." She pushed her chair back and rose. "Friday, October eighteenth."

"Right."

She went. My watch said 2:21. If she got names, I wouldn't enjoy *my* lemon-sherry pudding, so it was advisable to get that done, and I pushed the button and Mimi came. Her eyes went down to my plate and up to me. "You ate more than half of it, Mr. Goodwin. What do you think?"

"To be honest, Mimi, I don't know. When I've got a job on my mind I forget to taste. I'll have to come again."

She nodded. "I knew you were working on something, I can tell. Shall I do an omelet?"

I said no thanks, just the pudding and coffee, and she took my plate. In four minutes she was back, and I burned my tongue on the coffee because my stomach sent up word that it wanted help. Of course the pudding was no stranger. Mimi is good at puddings and parfaits and pastries. Also at coffee.

I was licking my spoon when Lily came, talking as she entered. "Don't get up. I got one name." She sat. "That woman is really low, I don't know why. He was twice her age, at least that, and I supposed she married him just to get in out of the rain. Didn't she?"

"I don't know, I never met her. You got a name?"

"Yes, just one. She said she didn't know who the others were, but one of them was a man she knew." She handed me a paper, light green, a sheet from her 5-by-8 memo pad. "She called him Benny. He's an engineer, with NATELEC, Bassett's company. More coffee?"

"No, thanks. You show promise. We'll raise your pay and—"

"I'll do better as I go along. You skip. You're not yourself when you'd rather be somewhere else." She picked up her spoon.

"I would *not* rather—I don't need to tell you what I'd rather."

I stood. "I'll tell you everything someday, and I hope you like it." I skipped.

In the elevator I looked at the slip. Benjamin Igoe. That was all, and I should have asked her how to pronounce it. On the sidewalk I stood for half a minute, then headed west and turned downtown on Madison. I had to decide how to handle it—using my intelligence guided by experience, as Wolfe put it. By Fifty-fifth Street it was decided, but my legs would get me there as soon as a taxi or a bus, so I kept going. It was five past three when the doorman at Rusterman's saluted and opened for me, so the lunch rush would be over and Felix could and would listen.

That was all he had to do, listen, except for pronouncing it. I spelled it, and he thought probably Eego, but I preferred Eyego, and since I had been born in Ohio and he had been born in Vienna, I won. When that was settled and he was thoroughly briefed, I went to the bar and ordered an Irish with water on the side. Even after the coffee my stomach still seemed to think something was needed, and I made it Irish to show Lily there was no hard feeling. Then I went and consulted the phone book for the address of National Electronics Industries. Third Avenue, middle Forties, which was a relief. It might have been Queens. I left by the side door.

They had three floors of one of the newer steel-and-glass hives. The directory on the lobby wall said Research and Development on the eighth, Production on the ninth, and Executive on the tenth. He might be anything from stock clerk to Chairman of the Board, but you might as well start at the top, so I went to the tenth but was told that Mr. Eyego was in Production. So I pronounced it right. On the ninth a woman with a double chin used a kind of intercom that was new to me and then told me down the hall to the last door on the right.

It was a corner room with four windows, so he wasn't a stock clerk, though you might have thought so from his brown overalls with big pockets full of things. He was standing over by a filing cabinet. I had never seen a more worried face. That might have been expected, since the president of his company had died only five days ago, but those brow wrinkles had taken at least five years. So it was a surprise when he said in a good strong baritone, "A message from Nero Wolfe? What the hell. Huh?"

My voice went up a little without being told to. "I said message, but it's really a question. It's a little complicated, so if you can spare a few minutes—"

"I can never spare a few minutes, but my mind needs something to take it off of the goddam problems. All right, ten minutes." He looked at his watch. "Let's sit down."

There was a big desk near a window, but that was probably where the goddam problems were, and he crossed to a couch over by the far wall. He sat and crossed his legs in spite of the loaded pockets, and I pulled a chair around to face him.

"I'll try to keep it brief, but you'll need a little background. For a couple of years Nero Wolfe was in charge of Rusterman's restaurant as trustee, and a man named Felix Mauer was under him. Now Felix is in charge, but he often asks Nero Wolfe for advice, and Mr. Wolfe and I often eat there. We ate lunch there yesterday, and Felix—"

"Huh. A waiter from that restaurant was killed in Wolfe's house, a bomb, and you found the body. Huh?"

"Right. That's why we were there yesterday, to ask questions. The waiter's name was Pierre Ducos, and he waited on you at dinner in an upstairs room at Rusterman's on Friday, October eighteenth. Twelve days ago. Harvey H. Bassett was the host. You remember it?"

"Of course I remember it. It was the last meal I ever ate with him."

"Do you remember the waiter?"

"I never remember people. I only remember diffractions and emissions."

"Mr. Wolfe and I knew Pierre well, and he knew us. When he came there late Monday night, he told me a man was going to kill him. He also told me about the dinner on October eighteenth, and he told me he saw one of the guests hand Bassett a slip of paper and Bassett put it in his wallet, and that was all. He said he wanted to tell Nero Wolfe the rest of it because he was the greatest detective in the world. I took him upstairs to a bedroom, and apparently you know what happened then, like a couple of million other people. Well, there you are. That dinner had been eleven days ago, and why did he tell me about that and about the slip of paper one of you handed Bassett? That's why I'm here, and it brings me to the question I want to ask: did you hand Bassett a slip of paper, and what was on it?"

"No. Huh."

"Did you see one of the others hand him one?"

"No. Huh." He seemed to be scowling at me, but it could have been just the wrinkles.

"Then I have to ask a favor, or rather Nero Wolfe does. We asked Felix who the guests were at that dinner, and the only one he could name was you. He said someone had told him who you were, Benjamin Igoe, the well-known scientist. I don't know if you like to be called a scientist, but that's what Felix was told."

"I don't believe it. Goddam it, I am *not* well known."

"Maybe you are and don't know it. That's what Felix told me. You can call him and ask him."

"Who told him that?"

"He didn't say. He's there now. Give him a ring." I thought he probably would, there and then. Nine men out of ten would have, or maybe only seven or eight.

But not him. He just said, "Huh. By god, if I'm famous it's about time I found out. I'm sixty-four years old. You want a favor?"

"Nero Wolfe does. I'm just the errand boy. He wants—"

"You're a licensed private investigator. Well known."

"You can't believe what you read in the paper. I am *not* well known." I wanted to say huh but didn't. "Mr. Wolfe wants the names of all the men who were at that dinner, but if you never remember people, of course you can't tell me."

"I remember the *names* of everything, including people." He proved it. "Did Pierre Ducos tell you what we talked about?"

I shook my head. "He only told me what I told you."

"We talked about tape recorders. That's what Harvey had us together for. Did you know Harvey Bassett?"

"No. Of course I had heard of him, he was well known too."

"I knew him all my life, most of it, we were at college together. He was three years older than me. I was a prodigy. Huh. No more. I took physics, and he took business. He made a billion dollars more or less, but up to the day he died he couldn't tell an electron from a kilovolt. Also he was unbalanced. He had obsessions. He had one about Richard Nixon. That was why he had us there. He made the equipment for electronic recording, or rather that was one of the things we made and he sold, and he thought Nixon had debased it. Polluted it. He wanted to do something about it but didn't know what. So he had us—"

He bit it off and looked at his watch. "Goddam it, twelve minutes." He jumped up, more like twenty-four than sixty-four. He moved, but I grabbed his arm and said firmly, "Goddam it, the names."

"Oh. Did I say I would?" He crossed to the desk, sat, got a pad of paper and a pen, and wrote, fast, so fast that I knew it wouldn't be legible. But it was. I had stepped over, and he tore it off and handed it to me, and a glance was enough. All five of them.

"Mr. Wolfe will be grateful," I said, and meant it. "*Damn* grateful. He never leaves his house, and almost certainly he will want to tell you so and have a talk. Is there any chance you would drop in on him, perhaps on your way home?"

"I doubt it. I suppose I might. My kind of work, I never know what I'm going to do. Huh. You get out of here."

Turning, I said, "Huh." I didn't really *say* it, it just came out. And I walked out.

Also I walked the ten blocks down to Thirty-fifth street and across town to the old brownstone. As I mounted the stoop it was half past four and Wolfe would be up in the plant rooms, and I hung up my coat and went to the office, sat, and looked at the list. He had written not only the names, but also what they did. If my time hadn't been up, he might have included ages and addresses. I tossed it on the desk and sat and looked at the picture. It was now an entirely new ballgame. By tossing Richard Nixon into that dinner party he had put a completely new face on it. Knowing Wolfe as I did, that was obvious. It was so obvious that it took me only ten minutes to decide what to do first, and I did it. I got at the phone and dialed a number.

It took more than half an hour to get all three of them. Actually I only got Fred; for Saul and Orrie I had to leave urgent messages. Then I pulled the typewriter around and made five copies of the list of names. I don't have to type it here for you because I already have. Then I typed the conversation with Igoe, verbatim, one carbon. I usually don't read things over, but I did that, and was on the second page when the elevator rattled coming down and clanked at the bottom, and Wolfe came.

He went to his desk and sat and said, "You're back." He rarely says things that are obvious, but he says that fairly often because it's a miracle that I'm not limping or bleeding after spending hours out in the concrete jungle.

"Yes, sir. I'll try to cover it all before dinner. I saw Felix and Lon Cohen and Miss Rowan and Felix again and one of the guests at that dinner named Benjamin Igoe, an electronics engineer with NATELEC, Bassett's company, and you'll want it all, but I prefer to give you the last one first. Igoe. I've typed my talk with him for the record." I swiveled to get it from my desk, swiveled again, and got up and handed it to him.

Three pages. He read the last page twice, looked at me with his eyes half shut, and said, "By God."

I stared at him. I may have gaped. He never says by god, and he said it with a capital G. So I didn't say anything.

He did. "Was he gibbering? Was it flummery?"

"No, sir. It was straight."

"He gave you their names."

"Right." It was in my hand, the one he had written, not a typed copy, and I passed it to him. He read it twice too. He put it down on his desk and then picked it up for another look. "I am not easily overwhelmed," he said. "If I could have them here now, all of them, I would pretermit dinner. I have occasionally asked you to bring people when I knew no one else could, but this—these six—not even you."

"I agree. So before I typed that conversation I did something. I used the telephone. More than once. And got results. You may have one guess."

He looked at me, straight, then closed his eyes. In about a minute, maybe a little more, he opened them and asked, "When will they come?"

"Nine o'clock. Fred sure, and Saul and Orrie probable. As you know, they like doing errands for you."

"Satisfactory," he said. "I'll taste my dinner. I haven't tasted food for two days."

7

I FORGET who once called them the Three Musketeers. Saul was in the red leather chair, and Fred and Orrie were in the two yellow ones I had moved up to face Wolfe's desk. Saul had brandy, Orrie had vodka and tonic, Fred had bourbon, I had milk, and Wolfe had beer.

Saul Panzer was two inches shorter, much less presentable with his big ears and unpressed pants, and in some ways smarter than me. Fred Durkin was one inch shorter, two inches broader, heavier-bearded, and in some ways a little more gullible. Orrie Cather was half an inch taller, a lot handsomer, and a little vainer. He was still sure he should have my job and thought it was conceivable that someday he would. He also thought he was twice as attractive to all women under forty, and I guess he was. He could say let's look at the record.

I had been doing most of the talking for more than an hour, and their notebooks were more than half full. I had given them the crop, saving nothing, with a little help from Wolfe in spots, but of course omitting irrelevant items such as the luncheon menu at Lily Rowan's. That had also been skipped when reporting to Wolfe before dinner. His real opinion of her wasn't anything near as low as he liked to pretend it was, but he didn't need another minus for her.

I took a sip of milk and said, "Now questions, I suppose."

"No," Wolfe said. His eyes moved left to right and back, to take them in. "I must first tell you the situation. Archie doesn't need to be told; he was aware of it before I was. What Mr. Igoe told him. He sees me every day, and hears me. He knew that for the first time in my life I had an itch that could not be relieved—that I hankered for something I couldn't get. He knew that I would have given all of my orchids—well, most of them—to have an effective hand in the disclosure of the malfeasance of Richard Nixon. I once dictated to him a letter offering my services to Mr. Jaworski, and he typed it, but it wasn't sent. I tore it up."

He picked up the bottle, decided not to pour, and put it down. "Well. Mr. Nixon is now out, no longer in command of our ship of state, no longer the voice of authority to us and of America to the world, but the record is by no means complete. History will dig at it for a century. It is now possible that I may be able to make a contribution. You heard what Mr. Igoe told Archie. Was he merely babbling, Archie?"

"No, sir. It was square."

"So I accept it and I expect you to. I trust Archie's eyes and ears, and I think you do. I am assuming that there was some connection between the name on that slip of paper, if it was a name, and the web of events and circumstances that is called Watergate; and further, that it resulted in the death by violence of Harvey Bassett and Pierre Ducos. Of Pierre, in this house. That's what I expect to establish, with your help. I have no client, so there will be no fee. Your usual rates will be paid, and of course expenses. I instruct you not to stint. It's nearing the end of a good year for me, even this year of a delirious economy, and it won't pinch me."

He sat straighter and palmed the chair arms. "Now. You have always trusted my judgment and followed instructions without question. Now you can't. I don't. On this I can't be sure my intellect will ignore the goad of my emotions. It may already have been gulled. The assumptions I have made—are they witless? I have asked Archie. Saul?"

"For a try, no."

"Fred?"

"No, sir."

"Orrie?"

"I agree with Saul. Good enough to work on."

Wolfe nodded. "I'm not convinced, but in any case I am going to get the man who killed Pierre—and might have killed Archie. But don't trust me blindly. If you doubt the soundness of my conclusions or instructions, say so. I would like to come out of this with my self-esteem intact, and so would you."

He leaned back. "To the job. If one of those six men is the culprit, he was with Bassett in an automobile last Friday night, and he had access to Pierre's coat Monday, day before yesterday, no matter what his motive was. To that the soundness of my assumptions is immaterial, and my emotions are not involved. Archie has given you lists of their names and has told you that five of them are in the Manhattan telephone directory. One of the lawyers, Mr. Ackerman, is in the Washington directory. Saul, you will start with the other lawyer, Mr. Judd. What is he? Where was he? Of course you won't ask *him*. If he learns you are inquiring about him, he may ask you, and if you need to consult with Archie, he will be here. Better Archie than me; on this I am suspect. As I said."

"Yes, sir. A question?"

"Yes?"

"You have told us not to follow your instructions without question. Lucile Ducos, Pierre's daughter. What Igoe said and the names he gave may have made you forget her." He looked at me. "You think he may have shown her the slip of paper?"

"*May* have, certainly."

"Could I open her up?"

"Possibly. If anybody could. I doubt it."

Back to Wolfe. "The name may not be one of those six men. It may have no connection with Watergate or Nixon. That may be why you forgot her. I could give it a try. Archie looks like a male chauvinist, and I don't."

Wolfe's lips were tight. He had asked for it, but even so it was hard to take. I am supposed to badger him, that's one of the forty-four things I get paid for, but not them, not even Saul.

"I'll discuss it with Archie," Wolfe said. "In asking about Mr. Judd, if you reveal that I sent you, so much the better. He may resent it and want to tell me so. Fred, you will start with Mr. Vilar. Since he deals with what is euphemistically called security, you will be familiar with those around him. My comments to Saul apply to you. Questions?"

"No, sir. Archie will be here?"

"Yes. He will see Mr. Igoe again and bring him if possible, but that will have to wait. At least he will be here tomorrow. Orrie, I believe you are known at Rusterman's."

"Well . . ." Orrie let it hang five seconds. "I have been there, sure. With my wife. Not often; I can't afford it."

"You were there two years ago, when money was taken from one of the men's lockers and Felix asked me to investigate. I sent you."

"Oh, that, sure."

"So you have seen that room, and many of the men have seen you. Pierre's coat could have been anywhere that he was that day or evening, but that room is the most likely. Was a stranger seen there that evening? Go and find out. Archie will tell Felix to expect you. Don't go until eleven o'clock, and interfere with the routine as little as possible. Have in mind another possibility, that the bomb was put in the coat by one of them. Archie and I think it unlikely, but it isn't excluded. You will not mention the slip of paper; you know what we promised Philip. Questions?"

Orrie shook his head. "About that, no. That's simple. And Archie will be here. But I'd like to say—about the ante. Fred has a family and needs it, but my wife has a good job with good pay, and we won't starve for a couple of weeks. Also I've got some feelings about Nixon too. If you pay the expenses, I'd like to donate my time."

"No." Wolfe clipped it. "This is my affair. When Archie said it's all in the family, he meant merely that I have no client. No."

"I live here," I said. "I took him up to that room. It's a family affair." Inside I was grinning. Orrie was so damn obvious. He thought my taking in a man with a bomb was a black mark for me, and offering to donate his time showed that he was fully worthy to step in when I stepped out. I'm not saying he was dumb. He wasn't.

Fred said, "Hell, I wouldn't starve either. I've got two families. I don't live here like Archie, but I like to think this is my *professional* family."

Saul said, "So do I. I raise. I'll pay expenses—mine."

Wolfe said, "Pfui. It's *my* affair. Archie, five hundred to each of them. There may be occasion to buy some facts. Record it as usual; it may be deductible, at least some of it."

I went and opened the safe, got the reserve cash box, and made three piles—ten twenties, twenty tens, and twenty fives, all used bills. When I finished, the members of the family were on their feet, including Wolfe. He had shaken hands with them when they arrived, but they didn't offer now because they knew he didn't like it. They took the bills and went to the hall for their coats.

When I returned to the office after letting them out and sliding the bolt, Wolfe had the list of names and the conversation with Igoe in his hand. Taking them up to bed with him. "Still half an hour to midnight," he said. "I'll sleep, and so will you. Good night."

I returned it and started collecting glasses and bottles.

8

AT A QUARTER PAST TEN Thursday morning I left the South Room and closed the door, which was no longer honored with the seal of the NYPD. Ralph Kerner, of Town House Services Incorporated, closed his imitation-leather-bound book and said, "I'll try to get the estimate to you by Monday. Tell Mr. Wolfe to expect the worst. That's all we get nowadays, the worst, from all directions."

"Yeah, we expect it and we get it. Isn't there a discount for a room where a man has just been murdered?"

He laughed. Always laugh at a customer's joke, even a bum one. "There certainly ought to be. I'll tell Mr. Ohrbach. So you took him up and left him." He laughed. "Good thing you left."

"It sure was. I may be dumb, but not that dumb."

Following him down the two flights, I would have liked to plant a foot on his fanny and push but controlled it.

The office chores were done, but I had been interrupted on a job of research—a phone call to Nathaniel Parker to ask for a report on the lawyers, Judd and Ackerman, one to our bank for a report on Hahn, the banker, and one to Lon Cohen about Roman Vilar, security, and Ernest Urquhart, lobbyist. I had enough on Igoe unless there were developments. Huh. Also one of the bottom shelves had seven directories, not counting the telephone books for the five boroughs and Westchester and Washington, and I had the *Directory of Directors* open at N to see if any of them were on the NATELEC list when Wolfe came down.

Three days' mail was on his desk, and he went at it. First, as usual, a quick once-through, dropping about half in the wastebasket. Of course I had chucked most of the circulars and other junk. He answers nearly all real letters, especially handwritten ones, because, he once told me, it is a mandate of civility. Also, I said, all he had to do was talk to me and he loved to talk, and he nodded and said that when he had to write them by hand he hadn't answered any. I said then he wasn't civilized, and that started him off on one of his hairsplitting speeches. We answered about twenty letters, three or four from orchid collectors and buffs as usual, with a few interruptions, phone calls from Parker and Lon Cohen and Fred Durkin. When I swiveled to my desk I was surprised to see him go to the shelves for a book—Fitzgerald's translation of the *Iliad*. In the mail there had been an inscribed copy of Herblock's new book, *Special Report,* with about a thousand cartoons of Nixon, but apparently he no longer needed to read or look at pictures about it because he was working on it. So he sat and read about a phony horse instead of a phony statesman.

He tasted his lunch all right. First marrow dumplings, and then sweetbreads poached in white wine, dipped in crumbs and eggs, sautéed, and doused with almonds in brown butter. I had had it at Rusterman's, where they call it *ris de veau amandine,* and Fritz's is always better. I know I haven't got Wolfe's palate. I know it because he has told me.

After lunch you might have thought we were back to normal. Theodore brought down a batch of statistics on germination and performance, and I entered them on the file cards. Week in and week out, that routine, about two per cent of which—the few he sells—applies to income and the rest to outgo, takes, on an average, about a third of my time. Wolfe, after listening to my reports on my morning's research, which contributed absolutely nothing, worked hard at comparing Fitzgerald's *Iliad* with the three other translations he brought over from the shelf. That was risky because they were on a high shelf and he had to use the stool. On the dot at four o'clock he left for the plant rooms. You might have thought we hadn't a care in the world. There hadn't been a peep from the members of the family. Wolfe hadn't even glanced at Herblock's *Special Report*. The only flaw was that when I finished typing the letters my legs and lungs wanted to go for a walk, and Saul and Fred and Orrie didn't have walkie-talkies.

At six o'clock the sound came of the elevator complaining as it started down, but it only lasted four seconds. He had stopped off for a look at the South Room, which he hadn't seen since one-thirty Tuesday morning. It was a good ten minutes before it started again, so he gave the ruins more than a glance. When he came and crossed to his desk and got settled, he said my guess of fifteen hundred dollars was probably too low with the bloated prices of everything from sugar to shingles, and I said I was glad to hear him having fun with words, tossing off an alliteration with two words that weren't spelled the same. He said it had been casual, which was a lie, and started reading and signing the letters. He always reads them, not to catch errors, because he knows there won't be any, but to let me know that if I ever make one it will be spotted.

It was ten minutes to seven and I was sealing the envelopes when the phone rang and I got it.

"Nero Wolfe's residence, Archie Goodwin speaking." Up to six o'clock it's "office." After six, "residence." I don't want people to think my nose is on the grindstone. Most offices close at five.

"May I speak to Mr. Wolfe, please? My name is Roman Vi*lar*. V-I-L-A-R."

I covered the mouthpiece and turned. "Fred has flushed one. Roman Vilar, euphemistic security. He asks permission to speak to Mr. Wolfe, please. Only he makes it Vi-*lar*."

"Indeed." Wolfe reached for his receiver. I kept mine.

"Nero Wolfe speaking."

"This is Roman Vilar, Mr. Wolfe. You have never heard of

me, but of course I have heard of you. But that isn't correct—you *have* heard of me, or at least your man Goodwin has. Yesterday, from Benjamin Igoe."

"Yes. Mr. Goodwin has told me."

"Of course. And he told you what Mr. Igoe told him. Of course. And Mr. Igoe has told me what he told Goodwin. I have told others, and they are here with me now in my apartment. Mr. Igoe and four others. May I ask a question?"

"Yes. I may answer it."

"Thank you. Have you told the police or the District Attorney what Mr. Igoe told Goodwin?"

"No."

"Thank you. Do you intend to? No, I withdraw that. I can't expect you to tell me what you intend to do. We have been discussing the situation, and one of us was going to go and discuss it with you, but we decided we would all like to be present. Of course not now—it's your dinnertime, or soon will be. Would nine o'clock be convenient?"

"Here. At my office."

"Certainly."

"You know the address."

"Certainly."

"You said four others. Who are they?"

"You have their names. Mr. Igoe gave them to Goodwin."

"Yes. We'll expect you at nine o'clock."

Wolfe hung up. So did I.

"I want a raise," I said. "Beginning yesterday at four o'clock. I admit it will be more inflation, and President Ford expects us to voluntarily lay off, but as somebody said, a man is worth his hire. It took me just ten minutes to get Igoe to spill that."

" 'The laborer is worthy of his hire.' The Bible. Luke. They offered to work for nothing, all three of them, and you want a raise, and it was you who took him up to bed."

I nodded. "And you said to me with him there on the floor and plaster all around him and on him, 'I suppose you had to.' "

Someday that will have to be fully discussed, but not now. We're talking just to show how different we are. If we were just ordinary people we would be shaking hands and beaming at each other or dancing a jig. It's your turn."

Fritz entered. To announce a meal he always comes in three steps, never four. But seeing us, when he stopped, what he said was, "Something happened."

Damn it, we were and are different. But Fritz knows us. He ought to.

Before going to the dining room I rang Saul's number, got his answering service, and left a message that I couldn't make it to the weekly poker game and give Lon Cohen my love.

9

THE ONLY VISIBLE evidence in the office that we had company was six men on chairs. Since this was a family affair, not business, it could be mentioned at the table, and after the cognac flames on a roast duck Mr. Richards had died, and Wolfe had carved it, and Fritz had brought me mine and taken his, we had discussed the question of setting up a refreshment table and had vetoed it. It would have made them think they were welcome and we wished them well, which would have been only half true. They were welcome, but we did not wish them well—at least not one of them.

To a stranger entering the office it's obvious at a glance that the red leather chair is the place. I had intended to put Benjamin Igoe in it, but a bishop with a splendid mop of white hair and quick gray eyes went to it even before he pronounced his name. Ernest Urquhart, the lobbyist. They all pronounced their names for Wolfe before they sat—the other five on two rows of yellow chairs facing Wolfe's desk, three in front and two back. Like this:

WOLFE

URQUHART

me

JUDD   ACKERMAN   VILAR

IGOE   HAHN

"I'm not really arrogant or impudent, Mr. Wolfe," Urquhart said. "I took this chair only because these gentlemen decided

that, since we are all willing talkers, it would be wise to name a
spokesman, and they chose me. Not that their tongues are tied.
Two of them are lawyers. I can't say with Sir Thomas More, 'and
not a lawyer among them.' "

Not a good start. Wolfe didn't like quoters, and he was down
on More because he had smeared Richard III. I was wondering
whether Urquhart was a lobbyist because he looked like a toler-
ant and sympathetic bishop, or looked like that because he was a
lobbyist. He had the voice for it, too.

"I have all night," Wolfe said.

"It shouldn't take all night. We certainly hope not. As you
must have gathered from what Mr. Vilar said on the phone,
we're concerned about what Mr. Igoe told Mr. Goodwin about
Mr. Bassett—and what Mr. Goodwin told him. Frankly, we think
it was unnecessary and indiscreet, and—"

"Leave that out! Goddam it, I told you." It was Igoe's strong
baritone, even stronger.

"That was understood, Ernie." Ackerman. Francis Ackerman, lawyer, Washington. I am not going to drag in Watergate,
it certainly doesn't need any dragging in by me, but when they
had single-filed in from the stoop he had struck me as a fairly
good take-off of John Mitchell, with his saggy jowls and scanty
chin. His calling Ackerman "Ernie" showed that he was the kind
of Washington lawyer who is on nickname terms with lobbyists.
Anyhow, one lobbyist.

Urquhart nodded. Not to Ackerman or Igoe or Wolfe; he just
nodded. "That slipped out," he told Wolfe. "Please ignore it.
What concerns us is the possible *result* of what Mr. Igoe told Mr.
Goodwin. And he gave him our names, and today men have been
making inquiries about two of us, and apparently they were sent
by you. Were they? Sent by you?"

"Yes," Wolfe said.

"You admit it?"

Wolfe wiggled a finger. That was regression—I just looked it
up. He had quit finger-wiggling a couple of years back. "Don't

do that," he said. "Calling a statement an admission is one of the oldest and scrubbiest lawyers' tricks, and you're not a lawyer. I state it."

"You'll have to make allowances," Urquhart said. "We are not only concerned, we are disturbed. Apprehensive. Mr. Goodwin told Mr. Igoe that at that dinner at Rusterman's one of us handed Mr. Bassett a slip of paper, and—"

"No."

"No?"

"He told Mr. Igoe that Pierre Ducos had *told him* that he had seen one of you hand Mr. Bassett a slip of paper. Also that that was the one fact that Pierre had mentioned, and that therefore we considered it significant."

"Significant of what?"

"I don't know. That's what I intend to find out. One week after that dinner Mr. Bassett was shot and killed. Ten minutes after Pierre told Mr. Goodwin that he saw one of you hand Mr. Bassett a slip of paper at that dinner—told him that and nothing else—he was killed by a bomb in this house. Mr. Urquhart, did you hand Mr. Bassett a slip of paper at that dinner?"

"No. And I want to make—"

"No is enough." Wolfe's head turned. "Did you, Mr. Judd?"

"No."

"Did you, Mr. Ackerman?"

"No."

"Did you, Mr. Vilar?"

"No. I am—"

"Did you, Mr. Hahn?"

"No."

"You told Mr. Goodwin no, Mr. Igoe. I ask you again. Did you?"

"Huh. No."

Wolfe's head went left and right to take them in. "There you are, gentlemen. Rather, there I am. Either Pierre lied to Mr. Goodwin or one of you lies. I don't think Pierre lied; why would he? Another question: did any of you see one of the others hand Mr. Bassett a slip of paper? I don't need another round of noes; I invite a yes. Any of you?"

No yes. Roman Vilar said, "We can't ask Pierre about it. He's dead." Vilar, euphemistic security, was all points—pointed chin, pointed nose, pointed ears, even pointed shoulders. He was probably the youngest of them—at a guess, early forties. His saying that they couldn't ask Pierre also pointed, for me, to the fact that when Wolfe had told me Wednesday morning what to say to them, or one of them, if I got the chance, I hadn't fully realized how much dust could be kicked up by one little lie. One more mention by anybody that Pierre had told me that he had seen one of them hand Bassett a slip of paper and I would begin to believe it myself.

"Yes," Wolfe said, "Pierre Ducos is dead. I saw him, on his back, with no face. I can't ask him either. If I could, almost certainly you would not be here, not all of you. Only one." He focused on Urquhart. "You said you are concerned not only about what Mr. Goodwin told Mr. Igoe but also about what Mr. Igoe told him. So am I. That's why I am having inquiries made about you—all of you. Mr. Igoe used the term 'obsession.' I don't have obsessions, but I too am attentive to the skulduggery of Richard Nixon and his crew. And the purpose of that gathering, arranged by Mr. Bassett, was to discuss it. Yes?"

"I suppose you might—"

"Hold it, Urquhart. Is this being recorded, Wolfe?"

Albert O. Judd, the other lawyer. He was about the same age as Vilar. He looked like a smoothie, but not the oily kind, and he had paid somebody a good four C's for cutting and fitting his light-gray coat and pants, the kind of fabric that suggests stripes but doesn't actually have any. Marvelous.

Wolfe eyed him. "You must know, Mr. Judd, that that question is cogent only if the one who asks it can rely on the one who answers, and why should you rely on me? It isn't to be expected that I'll say yes, and what good is my no? However, I say it. No."

His eyes took them in, from Judd around to Urquhart. "Mr. Vilar asked me on the telephone if I had told the police or the District Attorney what Mr. Igoe told Mr. Goodwin, and I said no. He asked me if I intended to but withdrew the question because he couldn't expect me to answer. But I *will* answer. Again no. At present I intend to tell no one. I do intend to learn who killed Pierre Ducos, and I have reason to surmise that in doing so I'll also learn who killed Harvey Bassett."

He turned a palm up. "Gentlemen. I know why you're here, of course. At present the officers of the law have no reason to assume that any of you were implicated in a homicide. Two homicides. Naturally they have inquired about Mr. Bassett's movements and activities immediately prior to his death, but he was a busy man of affairs, and they probably know nothing of that dinner a week earlier. If they knew what I know, they would not merely assume that one or more of you might be implicated; you would be the main focus of their investigation." He turned to me. "Your notebook, Archie."

I got it, and a pen. He had closed his eyes. He opened them to see that I was equipped, and closed them again. "Not a letterhead, plain paper. Merely a list of questions. How long had you known Mr. Bassett and what were your relations with him? Why were you included in a meeting called by him to discuss Richard Nixon's use or abuse of tape recorders? Did you know that Mr. Bassett felt that Mr. Nixon had debased and polluted tape recorders, comma, and did you agree with him? Have you ever been involved in any activity connected with the phenomena called Watergate, comma, and if so what and how and when? Have you ever had any contact with anyone connected with Watergate? To your knowledge, comma, even hearsay, comma, have any of the other five guests ever been connected in any way with Watergate, comma, and if so who? Where were you and what were you doing last Friday night, comma, October twenty-fifth, comma, from six p.m. to two a.m.? Where were you and what were you doing last Monday, comma, October twenty-eighth, comma, from twelve noon to twelve midnight?"

He opened his eyes. "Six carbons. No, only five, we won't need one. No hurry." He turned to them. "That, gentlemen, is a sample of the questions you are going to be asked. Either by me or by the police. You have a choice. You realize that—"

"This has gone far enough. Too far. Wolfe, I am a senior vice-president of the fourth largest bank in New York. We will pay you one hundred thousand dollars to represent our interests. One half tomorrow in cash, and the remainder guaranteed—probably by us jointly and certainly by me personally. Orally. Not in writing."

Willard K. Hahn's voice was soft and low, but the kind of soft and low you don't have to strain to hear. He was a square. He would have been obviously a square even without his square jaw and square shoulders—the opposite of Vilar with his points.

Wolfe was looking down his nose at him. "Not a good offer, Mr. Hahn. If as payment for services, too much. If as a bribe to muzzle me, not enough."

"It's for services. Too much? *You* saying too much, when you have just said we would be the main focus of a murder investigation? Vilar says you charge the highest fees in New York. If I need something, I buy it and I pay for it. I knew Harvey Bassett for twenty years. He was a good customer of my bank. And he's dead. Ben Igoe says he had an obsession about Richard Nixon and the tapes, and that's true, he did, but that wasn't his only obsession. When I heard of his death, how he died, my first thought was his wife—his obsession about *her*. Have you—"

"Goddam it, Hahn, you would!" Igoe's strong baritone. "You would drag her in!"

"You're damn right I would. *He* would drag her in, he always did, you know that, you ought to. Or he would drag her out." Back to Wolfe. "That slip of paper. If one of us handed him a slip of paper, it wouldn't have been about Nixon and tapes. That was what we were talking about, Nixon and tapes, why hand him a slip of paper, why not just say it? Evidently you think that slip of paper had something to do with his being murdered. If it did, it wasn't about tapes. I know nothing about it, I never heard of it until Ben Igoe told me what Goodwin told him, but when he did I— What did I say, Ben?"

"You said it was probably about Dora. Huh. You would."

"I think," Roman Vilar said, "that we should stick to what brought us here. That list of questions, Mr. Wolfe. You say they'll be asked either by you or by the police. Asked by you now? Here and now?"

"No," Wolfe said. "It would take a night and a day. I didn't invite you to come in a body; you invited yourselves. I intended to see you, but singly, after getting reports from the men I sent to make inquiries. I suggest that—"

"You won't see *me* singly." Ackerman, the Washington lawyer. He sounded like John Mitchell, too—at least the way Mitchell sounded on television. "You won't see me at all. I'm surprised that you don't seem to realize what you're trying to do. You're trying to get us to go along with you on a cover-up, and not a cover-up of a break-in to look at some papers, a cover-up of a murder. You say two murders. Of course I don't want to be involved in a murder investigation, nobody does, but at least I'm not guilty. But the way you're playing it, if I go along with you, I *would* be guilty. A cover-up of a murder. Obstruction of justice. Urquhart asked you if this is being recorded. I hope it is. When I talk to the District Attorney I would enjoy being able to tell him that this is on tape and he can—"

"No," Hahn, the banker, said. You wouldn't think such a low, soft voice could cut in, but it did. "You're not going to talk to the District Attorney or anyone else. I'm not a lawyer, but I don't think we'll be charged with obstruction of justice merely because a private detective told us that a man said something about a slip of paper, and I do *not* want to be involved in a murder investigation. I don't think any of us—"

Two or three voices, not soft and low, stopped him. I could try to sort it out and report it, but I won't because it wouldn't decide anything. Wolfe just sat and took it in. I got his eye and asked a question by pointing to my notebook and then the typewriter, but he shook his head.

But it did decide something. When it became obvious that they were all stringing along with Hahn, and Ackerman was a minority of one, Wolfe stopped the yapping by raising his voice.

"Please! Perhaps I can help. Mr. Ackerman is a member of the bar, and I am not, but his position is not tenable. Probably Watergate has made him excessively sensitive about cover-ups. Four lawyers have been disbarred, and more will be. But you can't be charged with obstruction of justice when all you have is hearsay. Perhaps *I* can be charged, but my taking that risk is of no concern to you. If Mr. Ackerman talks to the District Attorney, I'll be in a pickle, but he'll probably regret it, guilty or not."

He looked at the wall clock. "It's past ten o'clock. As I said, I must see each of you singly. Mr. Ackerman, you may want to get back to Washington. Why not stay now and let the others go?"

"No," Hahn said. "I repeat my offer. One hundred thousand dollars."

That started them off again, all of them but Ackerman and Vilar, and again I won't try to sort it out. But three of them got to their feet, and soon Urquhart left the red leather chair and made it four, and I got up and crossed to the door to the hall. Again there was a clear majority, and when Vilar and Igoe joined me at the door Wolfe spoke up.

"You will hear from me. All of you. From Mr. Goodwin. He will telephone and make appointments to suit your convenience —and mine. The best hours for me are eleven in the morning, six in the afternoon, and nine in the evening, but for this I would trim. I don't want to protract it, and neither do you. There will—"

I missed the rest because Igoe had headed for the front and I went to help with his coat and hat.

When all five of them were out and the door shut, and I re-

turned to the office, Ackerman was in the red leather chair, leaning back with his legs crossed. He was big and broad, and the
yellow chairs were much smaller. As I crossed to my desk he was
saying, ". . . but you don't know anything about me except that
I look like John N. Mitchell."

He not only admitted it, he even put the N in. I liked that.

"I have been told," Wolfe said, "that you are a reputable and
respected member of the bar."

"Certainly. I haven't been indicted or disbarred. I have had an
office in Washington for twenty-four years. I'm not a criminal
lawyer, so I haven't been invited to act for Dean or Haldeman or
Ehrlichman or Colson or Magruder or Hunt or Segretti. Or even
Nixon. Do you actually expect to put me through that catechism
you dictated?"

"Probably not. Why were you included in that gathering?"

"It's complicated. Albert Judd was and is chief counsel for
NATELEC. Five years ago he was acting on a tax matter for
them and needed a Washington man and got me. That's how I
met Harvey Bassett. Bassett thought he needed a good lobbyist,
and I got Ernest Urquhart, one of the best. I have known him for
years. He disappointed me here tonight. He is usually a wonderful talker, I *know* that, but I guess this wasn't his pitch. I had
never met the other three—Hahn, the banker, or Vilar, the security man, or Igoe. I knew Igoe is a vice-president of the corporation."

"Then you know nothing about Hahn's comment about Mrs.
Bassett. And Igoe."

I raised a brow. What did that have to do with Watergate and
tapes?

"No. Yes, nothing. I—" He flipped a hand. "Except hearsay."

"Whom did you hear say what?"

I have tried to talk him out of that "whom." Only highbrows
and grandstanders and schoolteachers say "whom," and he
knows it. It's the mule in him.

Ackerman's chin was up. "I'm submitting to this, Wolfe, only because of them. Especially Urquhart and Judd. Judd called me last night—Igoe had talked to him—and I took a plane to New York this morning and we had lunch. He told me things about Bassett that I hadn't known, and one of them was his—he didn't say 'obsession,' he said 'fix' about his wife. I don't peddle hearsay; you can ask Judd."

"I shall. Did you know how Bassett felt about Nixon and tapes?"

"Yes. A few months ago he and Judd were in Washington about some patents—I know something about patents—and we spent a whole evening on Nixon and tapes. Bassett had the wild idea that Nixon could be sued for damages—ten million dollars—for slandering and defaming manufacturers of electronic recorders by using them for criminal and corrupt purposes. We couldn't talk him out of it. He was a nut. I don't know if he was balmy about his wife, but he was about that. Of course that was a part of how he made it big in business—his drive. He had *that*."

"What was said—decided—about it at that meeting?"

"Nothing was decided. Bassett wanted Vilar to say that it was difficult to persuade corporation executives to contract for security appliances and personnel because they thought Nixon had given electronic equipment a bad name. He wanted Urquhart to say that if you tried to lobby for anybody connected in any way with electronics, no one on the Hill would listen to you. He wanted Igoe to say that men working in electronics—all levels, top to bottom—were quitting and you couldn't get replacements. He wanted Judd and me to say that all of that was actionable and we would act. God only knows what he wanted Hahn to do—maybe lend him a couple of million without interest to back the crusade."

Wolfe was eying him. "And you grown men, presumably sentient, soberly discussed that drivel? Or were you tipsy?"

"No. Judd and I hadn't even had martinis, because we knew Bassett would buy Montrachet and Château Latour. He always did. But you didn't know Harvey Bassett. He could sell ice cubes

to an Eskimo. Also, of course, he was a source of our income—
for at least two of them a major source—and you don't spit in the
eye of the source of your income. You take a bite of roast pheas-
ant and a sip of Latour and pretend to listen hard. Most men do.
I do. From what I've heard of you, maybe you don't."

"It's a matter of style. I have mine. I have due regard for my
sources of income. Is one—"

"Like me, you have different clients for different cases. Who's
your client in this one?"

"I am. Myself. I have had my nose pulled. Spat upon. Pierre
Ducos was murdered in a bedroom of my house. The man who
did it will pay. Is one—"

"Then why are you withholding evidence from the police?"

"Because it's *my* job. And it may not be evidence; I'm finding
out. I start a question the third time: Is one of your clients connected in any way with Watergate?"

"Everyone in Washington is connected in some way with Watergate. That's stretching it, but not much. The members of all
those juries have thousands of relatives and friends. No present
or former client of mine is or has been actually involved in Watergate. You're supposed to be asking the questions, but I'll ask
another one. Do you really believe one of us six men killed Harvey Bassett? Or was implicated in his murder or the other one?"

"Of course I do. I'm paying three men forty dollars an hour to
inquire about you. To your knowledge, have any of them been
connected in any way with Watergate?"

"To my knowledge, no. If I were Haldeman, I would say not
to my recollection, but I'm not Haldeman."

"Where were you and what were you doing last Friday night,
October twenty-fifth, from six p.m. to two a.m.?"

"By god, you ask it. I remember *because* that was the night
Bassett died. I was at home in Washington. From nine p.m. on I
was playing bridge with my wife and two friends until after midnight. I sleep late most Saturdays. At nine o'clock my wife woke
me to tell me that Bassett had been murdered. What was the

other one? Monday? I was at my office. In Washington. Next question."

Wolfe likes to say that no alibi is impregnable, but I hoped he wouldn't send me to crack that one. Wives and bridge-playing friends can lie, but there was Monday too, and for us that was the one we really wanted.

He looked at the wall clock. Eight minutes past eleven. "I'm short on sleep," he said. "Are you going to see the District Attorney?"

Ackerman shook his head. "You heard what they said, especially Judd. He agrees with you; all we have is hearsay—from you. I'll be short on sleep too. I'd like to make the midnight to Washington."

"Then you'll excuse me." Wolfe pushed his chair back and rose. "I'm going to bed." He headed for the door. Ackerman got up, told me, "He's a goddam freak," and walked out.

10

WHEN Wolfe came down to the office at eleven o'clock Friday morning, Roman Vilar was sitting in the red leather chair.

It had been a busy morning—for me—starting with the routine phone calls from the hired hands. I told them about the party we had had—that nothing had been learned to change the program, they were to carry on, Saul on Judd and Fred on Vilar. Orrie's day at Rusterman's had been a blank; no one had seen a stranger in the dump room Monday, day or night. Having been instructed by Wolfe—summoned on the house phone when I went to the kitchen for breakfast—I sicked Orrie on Benjamin Igoe.

There had been three phone calls. From Lon Cohen to say that they had been sorry not to get my usual contribution at the poker game—which was libel, since I win as often as he does and nearly as often as Saul Panzer—and to ask when I would spill a bean. From Bill Wengert of the *Times* to insinuate that he might let me have a short paragraph on page 84 if I would bring it gift-packaged, addressed to him personally. From Francis Ackerman in his Washington office to say that if Wolfe wanted to see him again, tell him a day in advance, and to warn us that our phone might be tapped or our office bugged. Watergate had certainly got on lawyers' nerves.

Not a peep from Cramer or the DA's office. I had got Roman Vilar the third try, a little before ten, and he said he would have to cancel two appointments to come at eleven, and he would.

I had also done the chores, including drawing a check for three grand for Wolfe to sign because the fifteen hundred had about cleaned out the reserve cash box, and clipping November 1 coupons from some municipal bonds—in the tidy pile in the upper compartment of the safe with its own lock. I made a face as I clipped, because the rate on those bonds was 5.2 per cent, and high-grade tax-exempt municipals then being issued returned close to 8 per cent. Life is no joke if you're in or above the 50-per-cent bracket, as Wolfe was. Equal to 15 per cent on your money, and you only have to clip coupons—or have Archie Goodwin do it if you're busy nursing orchids.

Roman Vilar was not just a security errand boy. Fred had told me that Vilar Associates was maybe the biggest and best-known outfit in industrial security, and on the phone I had to go through two secretaries to get him. And he didn't start the conversation by inviting questions, far from it. He offered Wolfe a job, and me too.

"Before we get onto Harvey Bassett and your problem," he said, "I'd like to make a suggestion. One of my associates suggested it when I told him I was coming here, and three of us discussed it. We have some good investigators on our staff—two of them are absolutely top drawer—but as my associate said, think what it would mean if we were going after a contract with a big corporation, if we could say that if a really tough situation turned up we would put our best man on it, Nero Wolfe. Think what just the *name* would do. Of course there would be a certain amount of work for you, not too much, we know how you feel about work, but the main thing will be the *name*. I don't have to tell you how famous you are, you know that, and that's not all. There is also Archie Goodwin. We want him too, and the starting figure will be a hundred and twenty thousand for you, ten thousand a month, and thirty-six thousand for Goodwin, three thousand a month. We would prefer a five-year contract, but it could be three years if you prefer that, or even an option to terminate it at the end of a year if you would rather have it that way. Starting the first of the year, two months from now, but of course we could announce it immediately. I can see it, nothing loud or flashy, just a simple one-sentence announcement: 'If a major problem arises, our Nero Wolfe will be available.' "

He was leaning forward in the chair, all his points pointing—chin, nose, ears. "Of course," he said, "I don't expect an immediate answer. You'll want to consider it. You'll want to find out about us. But it's a firm offer. I would sign a contract here and now."

"Yes," Wolfe said, "I'll want to find out about you. Where were you and what were you doing last Friday night, October twenty-fifth, from six p.m. to two a.m.?"

Vilar slid back in the chair. He grinned. "I didn't expect *that*."

Wolfe nodded. "A fair exchange. Near the end of my talk with Mr. Ackerman last evening he asked if I really believe one of you six men killed Harvey Bassett, and I said of course, I am paying three men forty dollars an hour to inquire about you. That isn't ten thousand dollars a month, but it's a thick slice. It shouldn't take a month. You're in the security business. Richard Nixon's main buoy, in his frantic effort to keep himself afloat, was his plea of national security. Have you been involved in any way with any of the phenomena included in the term 'Watergate'?"

"No."

"Have you had any connection with anyone who has been involved?"

"One of the technicians who examined that tape with an eighteen-and-a-half-minute gap has done some work for me. Look, Wolfe. In my business I don't answer questions, I ask them. Forget it. Where I was last Friday night, for instance. Go fly a kite. We should have gone along with Ackerman. I may go to the DA myself. Why don't *you?* Why did you turn Hahn down? What are you trying to sell?"

Wolfe wiggled a finger. Regression again. Watergate had really loosened his hinges. "I'm not selling anything, Mr. Vilar." Vi-*lar*. "I'm buying satisfaction. Harvey Bassett wanted you to say that Richard Nixon had made it harder for you to sell your services. Had he in fact made it easier?"

"Well." Vilar stood up, no rush, taking his time. He looked down at Wolfe. It gives you an edge to look down at a man. "Well," he said, "I'll go to the DA myself."

"I doubt it," Wolfe said. He turned to me. "What odds, Archie?"

I pursed my lips. "Four to one."

Back to Vilar. "I'll make it five to one. A hundred dollars to twenty that you won't."

Vilar turned and marched out. "Marched" is wrong. Marching takes good full steps, and his legs weren't long enough. I followed him out and to the front with the idea of asking for a raise, four grand a month instead of three, but decided it wasn't the right moment. Back in the office I told Wolfe, "Actually it's ten to one. He's the kind that lets out all his sail and then puffs to make his own wind."

His eyes narrowed at me. "Who wrote that? Or said it?"

"I did. I've been looking through that book you just bought, *The Southern Voyages,* by that admiral, and I feel nautical. Is Vilar a murderer?"

"No. Possibly Bassett, but not Pierre. He wouldn't risk getting that bomb. Security. Confound it, I doubt if any of them would; they have all submitted to the constraint of prudence. Do you agree?"

"No. One of them might have known where he could get hold of one without anybody knowing. And Igoe could probably make one himself."

He grunted. "He is of course a menace. There is only one object on earth that frightens me: a physicist working on a new trick. Pfui. Reports?"

"Nothing to start a crack. Orrie didn't get a glimmer at Rusterman's, and I gave him Igoe. Saul, Judd is so solid and upright and well liked that he'll probably get a monument. Fred, everybody has a good word for Vilar, but he suspects that if any of them had had enough to drink it would be a different story. Acker—"

"When they call at one, tell them to come at six."

"I already have. They aren't earning their pay and they know it. Ackerman called from Washington to warn us that we may be phoning or talking on tape. That check on your desk is for the cash box, it's low. The letter from Hewitt about a new orchid was mailed last Saturday. Six days from Long Island to Manhattan. Forty-two miles. I could walk it in one day."

He reached for the pile of mail, glanced through it, and got up and went to the kitchen. Lunch was to be spareribs with a red-wine sauce that used eight herbs and spices, and he wanted to be sure Fritz didn't skimp on the garlic. They disagree about garlic. Montenegro vs. Switzerland.

As a rule I keep personal matters out of these reports, but since you know that I had got to Benjamin Igoe through Lily Rowan, I should mention that I had called her twice to let her know that I had seen him and it had led to developments. That afternoon, after we had disposed of the spareribs and answered the mail and I had been to the bank to cash the check, and Wolfe had gone up for his afternoon session with the orchids, I rang her again, told her that I was still out of jail, and said that I would probably be free to spend the weekend as she had suggested if I would still be welcome.

"I'm pretty sure I could stand you for an hour," she said, "and then we'll see. Anyway I want to look at you. I just got back from lunch with Dora Bassett at her house, and she asked about you again. And she has never seen you. Have you got some kind of draw that doesn't even need wires? Electronic?"

"No. Do me a favor. Don't ever mention electronics in my hearing. I'm sick and tired of electronics. Two favors. Tell me what she asked about me."

"Oh, don't get ideas. Nothing personal. She just asked if I had seen you and had you found out who put the bomb in Pierre's coat, but of course she didn't call him Pierre, she said 'that man' or 'that waiter.' I have a right to call him Pierre. As you know, I think he was the best waiter that ever fed me. He remembered that I like my fork at the right of my plate after just one time."

But she didn't ask what or how or why or when, although she knew we were working on it. Incredible. I'd buy a pedestal and put her on it if I thought she would stay. She would either fall off or climb down, I don't know which.

Again at six o'clock, when Wolfe came down, there was someone in the red leather chair. Saul Panzer, and Fred and Orrie were in two yellow ones. For a change we all had martinis. Fred didn't like the taste of gin but he wanted to be sociable. Wolfe would ring for beer, but he didn't, and that was a bad sign. When he skips beer, have your raincoat and rubbers handy.

He sat and surveyed them. "Nothing?"

They nodded. Saul said, "Never have so many done so little. You and Archie have at least looked at them."

"And seen nothing. Nothing that helps. Now. Weekends are always difficult, and don't try. Archie won't be here. Resume Monday morning. Fred, you will continue with Mr. Vilar. He's uneasy, and you may learn why. Call Archie Monday morning as usual. Orrie. How many of them have you seen?"

"All but three. They weren't there. One busboy saw someone in that room Monday he had never seen before, but he has only been there a week and anyway he's not too bright. Also, most of them were cagey. They knew what I was after, about Pierre, and, like everybody else, they don't want to be dragged in on a murder case. It's just possible that you might get something if you saw all of them yourself, but I doubt it. I could bring them in batches."

Of course he knew Wolfe wouldn't. Neither Saul nor Fred would have said that. Wolfe ignored it. "You may as well continue with Mr. Igoe, but call Archie Monday morning. Saul. You could see Mr. Judd himself. Should you?"

Saul shook his head. "I doubt it. I even doubt if *you* should. I have covered him pretty well. You have seen him, here with the others."

"Yes. I suppose Archie has told you that Mr. Hahn offered to pay me a hundred thousand dollars. I'll have to see him myself. I have seen Mr. Ackerman, and Mr. Urquhart is in Washington. You suggested Wednesday evening that you should see Miss Ducos."

"I said I could give it a try. I said Archie looks like a male chauvinist and I don't."

"Yes. See her. She feeds facts to a computer at New York University. Will she go to work tomorrow, Saturday?"

"Probably not. I'll find out. I'll want to ask Archie about her." Saul turned to me. "Any suggestions?"

"If I were a male chauvinist pig in good standing I'd say you might try raping her. As I said, she has good legs."

"I'd like to have a try at her," Orrie told Wolfe. "And Saul would be better with Igoe. Igoe's very brainy. He's a Ph.D."

We looked at him, surprised. He was good with women all right, we all knew that, but suggesting to Wolfe—to Wolfe, not just to me—to switch an errand from Saul to him, that was a surprise.

Wolfe shook his head. "Saul offered first. Has Archie told you that two of them—Ackerman and Vilar—have threatened to go to the District Attorney? We don't think they will, but they might, and if they do we'll have a problem. Mr. Cramer's attention will be directed at those six men, and he will learn that I have sent you to inquire about them. You will be questioned. You know the stand Archie and I have taken with both Mr. Cramer and the District Attorney. That will be futile unless you take the same stand. Tell them absolutely nothing. Stand mute. You will probably be held as material witnesses, possibly even charged with obstruction of justice. Mr. Parker will of course arrange for your release on bail. It's conceivable that eventually you'll be on trial for a felony and convicted, but I'll do everything in my power to prevent it."

He tightened his lips, then: "I suggest an alternative. Either you stay and take the risk, or you leave the jurisdiction immediately. The country. Either Canada or Mexico. Of course, at my expense. If you go, you shouldn't delay. At once. Tonight."

"I'll stay," Fred said. "I've got an idea about Vilar."

"What the hell," Orrie said. "Of course we stay."

"I won't say that," Saul said, "but I want to say *something*." He said it to Wolfe. "I'm surprised, really surprised, that you thought we might go."

"I didn't," Wolfe said.

Nuts. Saul knew damn well he didn't. They were all just putting on a charade.

11

I ADMIT THAT, like everybody else, I like to think that I have hunches. For instance, the time that I was in the office of the head of a Wall Street brokerage firm and he brought in four members of his staff, and after talking with them five minutes I thought I knew which one of them had been selling information to another firm, and two weeks later he confessed. Or the time a woman came and asked Wolfe to find out who had taken her emerald and ruby bracelets, and when she left I had told him she had given them to her nephew, and he had taken it on anyhow because he wanted to buy some orchid plants, and had regretted it later when he had to sue to get his fee. By the way, that was one of the reasons he thought I could size up any woman in ten minutes.

But I'm not going to say it was a hunch I had that Saturday morning, because I don't see how it could have been. It might have been just something I had for breakfast, but I don't see how that was possible either, because Fritz had catered it as usual.

Whatever caused it, I had it. When I am dressing and getting packed for a weekend at Lily Rowan's pad in Westchester, which she calls The Glade, I thoroughly approve of the outlook. I enjoy shaving. I think my hair looks fine, and my zipper works like a dream. I'm willing to admit that being away from him for forty-eight hours is a factor—a change is good for you—but also I would breathe some fresh air and so forth.

But not that time. The electric shaver was too noisy. My

fingers didn't like the idea of tying shoestrings. The tips of my necktie didn't want to come out even. I could go on, but that's enough to give you the idea. However, I made it. At least I didn't trip going downstairs.

Lily was expecting me out in front with the Heron at eleven o'clock, and it was only ten-twenty-five and there was no hurry, so I put my bag down in the hall, went to the kitchen to tell Fritz I was off, and to the office for a glance around. And as I was trying the knob of the safe, the phone rang. I should have left it to Fritz, but habit is habit, and I went and picked it up. "Nero Wolfe's resid—"

"I want to ask you just one question." Lon Cohen.

"If it can be answered yes or no, shoot."

"It can't. Where and when did you last see Lucile Ducos alive?"

I couldn't sink onto my chair, because it was turned wrong. I kicked it to swivel it and sat on the edge. "I don't believe it. Goddam it, I do *not* believe it."

"Yeah, they always say that. Are your eyes pop—"

"Quit clowning. When?"

"Forty minutes ago. We've just got a flash. On the sidewalk on Fifty-fourth Street a few yards from the house she lived in. Shot somewhere in the middle. Freebling is there, and Bob Adams is on the way. If—"

I hung up.

And my hand started for it to pick it up again. Actually. To pick it up and ring Homicide South to ask questions. Of course I pulled it back and sat and stared at it, first with my jaw set and then with my mouth open. Then I shut my eyes and my mouth. Then I did pick the phone up and dialed a number.

After six rings: "Hello?"

"Me. Good morning, only it isn't. Just as I was leaving, Lon Cohen phoned. There has been another murder, less than an hour ago. Lucile Ducos, Pierre's daughter. I'm stuck. I'm worse than stuck, I'm in up to my neck, and so is Wolfe. I hope you have a nice weekend. We don't say 'I'm sorry,' so I won't say it and neither will you. I'll think of you every hour on the hour. Please think of me."

"I don't ask if I can do anything, because if I could, you would tell me."

"I sure would. I will."

We hung up. I sat another three minutes, and then I got up and went and mounted the three flights to the plant rooms, taking my time. That was the third time, or maybe the fourth, I went down the aisles through those three rooms—the cool, then the moderate, then the warm—without seeing a thing. The benches could have been empty.

In the potting room Theodore was sitting at his little desk, writing on his pad of forms, and Wolfe was standing at the long bench, inspecting something in a big pot—presumably an orchid plant, but at that moment I wouldn't have known an orchid from a ragweed. As I crossed over he turned and scowled at me and said, "I thought you had gone."

"So did I. Lon Cohen phoned. Lucile Ducos was shot and killed about an hour ago on the sidewalk a few steps from her house. That's all Lon knew."

"I don't believe it."

"That's exactly what I said. I didn't either until I sat and went through the multiplication table. I beg your pardon for breaking a rule and interrupting you up here."

"Confound it, go."

I nodded. "Of course. Also of course Stebbins will be there and will take me down. You probably won't see me for—"

"No. Go to the country. Have your weekend. Tell Fritz to put the bolt on and ignore the telephone. I'll call Saul and tell him to call Fred and Orrie."

"Uhuh. You haven't sat and thought. For you two minutes should be enough. If the white apron—the maid—if she hasn't talked, she will. They'll know we were there. They'll know she found me in Lucile's room. They'll know Lucile sat and watched me for an hour while I did Pierre's room. So I know things about her they should know, and what I know, of course you know. If I disappear for the weekend and you bolt the door and don't answer the phone, that will only make it worse. I have phoned Miss Rowan."

Up there, when he sits it's usually on one of the stools at a bench, but there's a chair nearly big enough over in a corner, and he crossed to it. Since he hates to tilt his head to look up at someone standing, I went and got one of the heavy boxes for shipping plants in pots and brought it over and sat.

"It's Saturday," he said.

"Yes, sir. Parker will be somewhere playing golf, and even if I found him, judges won't be available, and Coggin almost certainly has still got those warrants. If you want to sleep in your house tonight, you have got to count ten and consider letting go. Don't scowl at *me*. I'm not trying to sell it, I'm not even suggesting it, I'm just telling you where I was when I finished the multiplication table. It seemed to me that even if we unloaded we could still go right on making inquiries about the commission of a capital crime on our private premises."

He growled, "You *are* trying to sell it."

"I am not. I'm game if you are. It's eleven o'clock, time to go down anyway, so come and sit in that chair and lean back and shut your eyes and work your lips. Cramer may be on his way here now. If not, he soon will be, and he may actually have handcuffs. We have been getting away with murder, and you know it and he knows it. Now three murders, because if the white apron is talking he knows about that dinner and the slip of paper Pierre did not tell me about."

He got up and walked out. Marched out. He always moves as if he weighed a twelfth of a ton instead of a seventh. When the door to the warm room had closed behind him, Theodore said, "It's always bad when you come up here."

I concede that as an orchid man Theodore may be as good as he thinks he is, but as a boon companion—a term I once looked up because Wolfe told me it was trite and shouldn't be used—you can have him. So I didn't bother to answer, and I would have liked to leave the box there for him to put back where it belonged, but that would have been like him, not me, so I didn't. I picked it up and returned it before leaving.

Wolfe had of course taken the elevator. When I entered the office he was standing over by the big globe, slowly turning it. Probably deciding where he wished he was, maybe with me along. I went to my desk and sat and said, "When Saul or Fred or Orrie hears the news he'll probably call, especially Saul. If so, what do I tell him?"

He turned the globe a few inches with his back to me. "To call Monday morning."

"He may be in the can Monday morning."

"Then call when Mr. Parker has got him out."

I got up and marched out. To the stairs and up to my room. One, the desire to kick his ample rump was so strong it was advisable to go where I couldn't see him, and two, what I had put on for a weekend in the country was not right for a weekend where I might spend it. While I got out more appropriate items and stripped, I tried to remember a time when he had been as pigheaded as this and couldn't. Then there must be a reason, and what was it? I was still working on that and putting on one of my oldest jackets when the phone rang and I went and got it.

"Nero Wolfe's—"

"You there, Archie? I thought you were going—"

"So did I. I got a piece of news." Saul Panzer. "Evidently you did too."

"Yes. Just now on the radio. I thought you were gone and he might need something."

"He does. He needs a kick in the ass and I was about to deliver it, so I came upstairs. I asked him what to say if you called, and he said tell you to call Monday morning."

"No."

"Yes."

"My god, doesn't he realize the cat's loose?"

"Certainly. I remarked that if he wanted to sleep here tonight he'd have to unload, and he just scowled at me. What did the radio tell you?"

"Only that she got it and the police are investigating. And that she was the daughter of Pierre Ducos. I called not only to ask if he needed something but also to report. I phoned her this morning at nine o'clock and told her that Nero Wolfe wanted me to see her and ask her a couple of questions. She said go ahead and ask them, and I said not on the phone, and she said to call her around noon. When I called at nine o'clock a woman answered, I suppose the one you call the white apron, and I told her my name and I was working for Nero Wolfe."

"Good. That helps. That makes it even better. You'd better stick a toothbrush in your pocket."

"And a couple of paperbacks to read. If I'm going to stand mute I'll have plenty of leisure."

"Happy weekend," I said and hung up.

There's a shelf of books in my room, my property, and I went to get one—I don't know why, since I wasn't in a mood for any book I had ever heard of—but realized that Fritz was probably wondering what the hell was going on. So I left, descended the two flights, and turned right at the bottom instead of left. In the kitchen Fritz was at the big table doing something to something. Normally I would have noticed what, but not that time. All the walls and doors on that floor are soundproofed, so I don't know why he wasn't surprised to see me. He merely asked, "Something happened?"

I got on a stool. "Yes, and more to come. A woman got killed, and it should mean a change of program, but he's trying to set a new world record for mules. Don't bother about lunch for me, I'll chew nails. I know you have problems with him too, garlic and juniper berries and bay leaf, but—"

The doorbell. I slid off the stool, went to the hall, took one look through the one-way glass panel, and entered the office.

Wolfe was at his desk with the middle drawer open, counting beer-bottle caps.

"Sooner even than I expected," I said. "Cramer. Saul called. He phoned Lucile Ducos at nine o'clock this morning. The maid answered and he told her his name and said he was working for you. He told Lucile Ducos he wanted to see her and ask her some questions, and she told him to call her around noon."

The doorbell rang.

He said, "Grrrhh."

"I agree. Do I let Cramer in?"

"Yes."

I went to the front and opened the door, swung it wide, and he stepped in. I stood on the sill and looked out and down. His car was double-parked, with the driver in front at the wheel and one in the back seat I had seen but had never met. When I turned, no Cramer. I shut the door and went to the office. He was standing at the edge of Wolfe's desk, his hat and coat on, talking.

". . . and I may sit down and I may not. I've got a stenographer out in the car. If I bring him in, will you talk?"

"No."

"It's barely possible that I have news for you. Do you know that Pierre Ducos's daughter was shot down in front of her house four hours ago?"

"Yes."

"You do. The old man still won't talk, in *any* language, but a Homicide Bureau man and I have just spent an hour with Marie Garrou, the maid. *Will* you talk?"

"No."

"Goddam it, Wolfe, what's eating you?"

"I told you three days ago that I was outraged and out of control. I am no longer out of control, but I am still outraged. Mr. Cramer. I respect your integrity, your ability, and your understanding. I even trust you up to a point; of course no man has complete trust in another, he merely thinks he has because he needs to and hopes to. And in this matter I trust only myself. As I said, I am outraged."

Cramer turned his head to look at me, but he didn't see me. He turned back to Wolfe and leaned over to flatten his palms on the desk. "I came here with a stenographer," he said, "because I trust you too, up to a point. I want to say something not as Inspector Cramer or Mr. Cramer to a private investigator or Mr. Wolfe, but just as Cramer to Wolfe. Man to man. If you don't let go, you're sunk. Done. Let me bring him in and talk to *me*. *Now.*"

Wolfe shook his head. "I appreciate this. I do. But even as Wolfe to Cramer, no."

Cramer straightened up and turned and went.

When the sound came of the front door opening and closing, I didn't even go to the hall for a look. If he had stayed inside, all right, he had. I merely remarked to Wolfe, "About any one little fact, I never know for sure whether you have bothered to know it or not. You may or may not know that the Homicide Bureau is a bunch of cops that don't take orders from Cramer. They're under the DA."

"Yes."

So he might have known it and he might not. "And," I said, "one of them helped him buzz Marie Garrou. I now know her name. And Cramer came straight here because he was sorry for you. That's hard to believe, but he did, and you should send him a Christmas card if you're where you can get one."

He squinted at me. "You changed your clothes."

"Certainly. I like to dress properly. This is my cage outfit. Coop. Hoosegow."

He opened the drawer, slid the bottle caps into it, shut the drawer, pushed his chair back, rose, and headed for the door. I supposed to tell Fritz to hurry lunch, but he turned right, and the elevator door opened and closed. Going up to tell Theodore to come tomorrow, Sunday. But I was wrong again; it went up only one flight. He was going to his room to change to *his* cage outfit, whatever that might be. It was at that point that I quit. The only possible explanation was that he really had a screw loose, and therefore my choice was plain. I could bow out for good, go to Twentieth Street, to either Stebbins or Cramer, and open the bag, or I could stick and take it as it came. Just wait and see.

I don't know, actually, why I stuck. I honestly don't know. Maybe it was just habit, the habit of watching him pull rabbits out of hats. Or maybe it was good old-fashioned loyalty, true-blue Archie Goodwin, hats off everybody. Or maybe it was merely curiosity; what *was* eating him and could he possibly get away with it?

But I know why I did what I did. It wasn't loyalty or curiosity that sent me to the kitchen to get things from the refrigerator—just plain horse sense. It would probably be Coggin, and he would like it even better if we were just sitting down to lunch, and I had had enough of the sandwiches they brought you at the DA's office. As I got out sturgeon and bread and milk and cucumber rings and celery and brandied cherries, Fritz looked but said nothing. He knows it is understood that it's his kitchen, and if I take liberties without asking, it is not the moment for conversation. My copy of the *Times* was still in the rack on the little table, and I opened it to Sports. I felt sporty. I was on the cherries when the sound came of the elevator. When I went to the office Wolfe was at his desk with a crossword puzzle.

I admit I have been working up to a climax, and here it is. Wolfe *had* gone up to change. But he had changed not to his oldest suit but his newest one—a soft light-brown with tiny yellow specks that you could see only under a strong light. He had paid Boynton $345.00 for it only a month ago. The same shirt, yellow of course, but another tie, solid dark-brown silk. I couldn't see his shoes, but he had probably changed them too. As I went to my desk and sat, I was trying to prepare a suitable remark, but it didn't come because I knew I should have just learned something new about him, but what?

"The mail," he said.

I hadn't opened it. I reached to my desk tray, a hollowed-out slab of green marble, for the opener and began to slit, and for the next twenty minutes you might have thought it was just a normal weekday. I had my notebook and Wolfe was starting on the third letter when Fritz came to announce lunch, and Wolfe got up and went without a glance at me. I don't know how he knew I had had mine.

I had typed the two letters and was doing the envelopes when the doorbell rang. My watch said 1:22, and the clock agreed. Evidently Coggin knew that Wolfe's lunch hour was a quarter past one. I got up and went. But it wasn't Coggin. It was a pair I had never seen before, standing stiff-backed shoulder to shoulder, and each one had a folded paper in his hand. When I opened the door, the one on the right said, "Warrants to take Nero Wolfe and Archie Goodwin. You're Goodwin. You're under arrest."

"Well," I said, "come in. While we get our coats on."

They crossed the sill and I shut the door. They were 5 feet 11, 180 pounds, very erect. I say "they" because they were twins, long narrow faces and big ears, but one was white and the other one black. "I've had my lunch," I said, "but Mr. Wolfe has just started his. Could we let him finish? Half an hour?"

"Sure, why not?" White said and started shedding his coat.

"No hurry at all," Black said.

They took their time hanging up their coats. No hats. I showed them the door to the office and entered the dining room. Wolfe was opening his mouth for a forkful of something. "Two from the Homicide Bureau," I said. "With warrants. I'm under arrest. I asked if you could finish your lunch, and they said sure, no hurry."

He nodded. I turned and went, in no hurry, in case he wished to comment, but he didn't. In the office, White was in the red leather chair with Wolfe's copy of the *Times,* and Black was over at the bookshelves looking at titles. I went to my desk, finished the envelopes and put things away, picked up the phone, and dialed a number. Sometimes it takes ten minutes to get Lon Cohen, but that time it took only two.

"So you're still around," he said.

"No. Here's that one little bean I said I would spill. Maybe in time for today. A scoop. Nero Wolfe and Archie Goodwin are under arrest as material witnesses. Just now. We are being taken down."

"Then why are you making phone calls?"

"I don't know. See you in court."

I hung up. Black said, "You're not supposed to do that." He was on a yellow chair with a book.

"Of course not," I said, "and I wonder why. 'No hurry at all.' I'm just curious. Do you feel sorry for me? Or for Nero Wolfe?"

"No. Why the hell should we?"

"Then you don't like the guy who sent you."

"Oh, he'll do. He's not the best but he's not the worst."

"Look," White said, "we know about you. Yeah, you're curious, more ways than one. Just forget it. It's Saturday afternoon, and we're off at four o'clock, and if we don't get there too soon we'll *be* off. So there's no hurry. If you have no objection."

He turned to another page of the *Times*. Black opened his book; I couldn't see the title. I got my nail file from the drawer and attended to a rough spot on my right thumbnail.

It was twenty-five minutes past two when we descended the seven steps of the stoop and climbed into the cars, Wolfe with White and me with Black.

12

STAND MUTE" sounds simple, as if all you had to do is keep your mouth shut, but actually it's not simple at all. Assistant District Attorneys have had a lot of practice using words. For instance:

"Why did you compel, physically compel, Lucile Ducos to stay with you in her father's room while you searched the room?"

"In the signed statement you gave Sergeant Stebbins you said you included everything Pierre Ducos said to you. But you left out that he saw one of the men at that dinner hand Bassett a slip of paper. Why did you tell that lie?"

"If Ducos didn't tell you who had been at that dinner meeting, how did you learn about Benjamin Igoe?"

"If Ducos didn't tell you about that dinner meeting, who did?"

"Why did you tell Saul Panzer that Lucile Ducos must be kept from talking?"

"When did you learn that Nero Wolfe had persuaded Léon Ducos not to talk to the police?"

"What did you take from the pockets of Pierre Ducos before you reported your discovery of his body?"

"What did you find concealed in a book in the room of Lucile Ducos?"

That's just a few samples. I haven't included a sample of some asked by an assistant DA I had never seen before, a little squirt with gold-rimmed cheaters, because they were so damn ridiculous you wouldn't believe it—implying that Nero Wolfe had opened up. Implying that Saul and Fred and Orrie had talked, sure, that was routine. But Wolfe—now, really. As for me, I don't suppose I set a record for standing mute, but between three o'clock Saturday afternoon and eleven-thirty Monday morning I must have been asked at least two thousand questions by three assistant DAs and Joe Murphy, the head of the Homicide Bureau. Most of Murphy's questions had nothing to do with murder. He wanted to know exactly why it had taken so long for Wolfe and me to get our coats on Saturday afternoon, and how the *Gazette* had got the news in time for the late edition that day. It was a pleasure to stand mute to him because I was glad to give Black and White a break, but with the others it wasn't easy and my jaw got tired from clamping it. The trouble was I like to be quick with good answers, and they knew it and did their best to get me started, and two of them were good at it. But mute doesn't mean pick and choose, it means mute, tongue-tied, aphonous, and don't forget it.

Of the lock-ups I have slept in, including White Plains, only thirty miles away, New York is the worst. The worst for everything—food, dirt, smell, companionship, prices of everything from newspapers to another blanket—everything. I hadn't seen Wolfe. I will not report on my feelings about him during that fifty-one hours, except to say that they were mixed. It was harder on him than on me, but he had asked for it. I hadn't used my right to make one phone call to ring Nathaniel Parker because I assumed Wolfe had, and anyway Parker had certainly seen the Sunday *Times,* no matter where he was. But where was he now? "Now" was ten minutes to six Monday afternoon, and I sat on my cot trying to pretend I wasn't stewing. The point was, at least one point, that tomorrow would be Election Day and judges might not be available—another reason to stew: an experienced private detective should know how many judges are available on Election Day, and I didn't. I was thinking that, in addition to everything else, Election Day had to come up and I might not be able to vote for Carey, when footsteps stopped at my door, a key scraped in the lock, the door opened, and a stranger said, "You're wanted downstairs, Goodwin. I guess you'd better take things."

There wasn't much to take. I put what there was in my pockets and walked out. My next-door neighbor on the left said something, but he was always saying something, and I didn't listen. The stranger herded me down the hall to the door at the end with steel bars about the size of my wrist, on which he had to use a key, on through, and across to the elevator. As we waited for it to come, he said, "You're number two hundred and twenty-four."

"Oh? I didn't know I had a number."

"You don't. *My* number. Guys I've had that I seen their pitcher in the paper."

"How many years?"

"Nineteen. Nineteen in January."

"Thanks for telling me. Two hundred and twenty-four. An interesting job you've got."

"*You* call it interesting. It's a job."

The elevator came.

In a big room on the ground floor with ceiling lights that glared, Nathaniel Parker sat on a wooden chair at one end of a big desk. The man behind the desk was in uniform, and another one in uniform stood at the other end. As I crossed over, Parker got up and offered a hand and I took it. The one standing pointed to a little pile of articles on the desk, handed me a 5-by-8 card, and said, "If it's all there, sign on the dotted line. There's your coat on the chair."

It was all there—knife, key ring, wallet with no money in it because I had it in my pocket. Since I had been standing mute, I made sure the card didn't say anything it shouldn't before I signed. My coat smelled of something, but I smelled even worse, so what the hell. Parker was on his feet, and we walked out. The one behind the desk hadn't said a word. Neither did Parker until we were out on the sidewalk. Then he said, "Taxis are impossible, so I brought my car. It's around the corner."

I said firmly, "Also there's a bar around the corner." My voice sounded funny, probably rusty and needed oil. "I'd like to hear you talk a little, and not while you're driving."

The bar was pretty full, but a couple were just leaving a booth and we grabbed it. Parker ordered vodka on the rocks, and when I said a double bourbon and a large glass of milk he raised his brows.

"Milk for my stomach," I told him, "and bourbon for my nerves. How much this time?"

"Thirty thousand. Thirty for Wolfe and the same for you. Coggin pushed hard for fifty thousand because you're implicated, so he says, and you're standing mute. He said the charge will be changed to conspiracy to obstruct justice, and of course that was a mistake, and Judge Karp called him. You don't go to court with a *threat*."

"Where's Wolfe?"

"At home. I took him an hour ago. I want to know exactly what the situation is."

"It's simple. There have been three murders, and we're standing mute."

"Hell, I know that. That's all I know. I have never known Wolfe like this. He's practically standing mute to *me*. I'm counting on you to tell me exactly where it stands. In confidence. I'm your counsel."

The drinks came, and I took a sip of milk and then one of bourbon, and then two larger sips. "I'll tell you everything I know," I said. "It will take an hour and a half. But I can't tell you why we've dived into a foxhole because I don't know. He's standing mute to me too. We could give them practically everything we've got and still go right on with our knitting—we've done that a thousand times, as you know—but he won't. He told Roman Vilar—you know who he is?"

"Yes. He told me that much."

"He told him he's buying satisfaction. Goody. He'll pay for it with our licenses. Of course—"

"Your licenses have been suspended."

"We won't need them if we're behind bars. Where are Saul and Fred and Orrie?"

"They're behind bars now. I'll get them out tomorrow morning. Judge Karp has said he'll sit. You honestly don't know why Wolfe has holed in?"

"Yes, I don't. You're my lawyer?"

"Of course."

"Then I can give you a privileged communication. Have you got an hour?"

"No, but go ahead."

I took a swallow of bourbon and one of milk. "First a question. If I tell you everything as your client, I'll also be telling you things about your other client that he is *not* telling. What about conflict of interest? Should I get another lawyer?"

"Not unless you want a better one. He knows I'm acting for you. He knows you can tell me anything you want to. If he's willing to risk a conflict of interest, it's up to you. Of course, if you *want* another lawyer—"

"No, thank you. You'll be famous. It's a coincidence—Wolfe will like that. Five men being tried now in Washington for conspiracy to obstruct justice—Haldeman, Ehrlichman, Mitchell, Mardian, and Parkinson. Five being charged here with conspiracy to obstruct justice—Wolfe, Goodwin, Panzer, Durkin, and Cather. That's probably what Wolfe has in mind. I'm glad to be in on it. So here's my privileged communication."

I drank, milk and then bourbon for a change, and proceeded to confide in my lawyer.

An hour and a half later, at five minutes past eight, Parker dropped me off at Thirty-fifth Street and Eighth Avenue. I would stretch my legs for a block and a half. He now had plenty of facts but could offer no suggestion on what to do with them, since I still intended to hang on. It was ten to one that he would have liked to advise me to turn loose but couldn't on account of Wolfe. That looked to me a lot like conflict of interest, but I had learned not to try splitting hairs with a lawyer. They think you're not in their class. Anyway we shook hands before I climbed out.

At the brownstone the chain bolt was on and I had to ring for Fritz. I am not rubbing it in when I say that he pinched his nose when I took my coat off; a super cook has a super sense of smell.

"I don't need to say," he said. "Anyway, here you are, *grâce à Dieu.* You look terrible."

I kept the coat on my arm. "I feel worse. This will have to go to the cleaners, and so will I. In about two hours I'll come down and clean out the refrigerator and shelves for you, and you can start over. He's in the dining room?"

"No, I took up a tray, a plain omelet with five eggs and bread for toast, and coffee. Before that he had me rub lilac vegetal on his back. The paper said you were in jail, all of you. Are you going to tell me anything? He didn't."

"It's like this, Fritz. I know ten thousand details that you don't know, but the one important detail, what's going to happen next —I'm no better off than you are. You tell *me* something. You know him as well as I do, maybe better. What's the French word for crazy? Insane. Batty."

"Fou. Insensé."

"I like *fou.* Is he *fou?"*

"No. He looked me in my eye."

"Okay, then wait and see. Do me a favor. Buzz him on the house phone and tell him I'm home."

"But you'll see him. He'll see you."

"No he won't. I'm not *fou* either. *You'll* see me in two hours."
I headed for the stairs.

13

YOU WOULD EXPECT—anyway, I would—that
the main assault in the campaign of the media to get the story to
the American people would come from the *Gazette*. The *Gazette*
was the leader in emphasizing flavor and color in everything
from markets to murders, and also there was the habit of my
exchanging tits for tats with Lon Cohen. But the worst two were
Bill Wengert of the *Times* and Art Hollis of CBS News. Now
that the dinner party at Rusterman's was in the picture—nobody
knew exactly how—and the murder of Harvey H. Bassett of
NATELEC was connected with the other two—nobody knew exactly why—probably the brass at the *Times* was on Wengert's
neck. And Hollis, the damn fool, had sold CBS the idea of sending a crew with equipment to Nero Wolfe's office for a twenty-
six-minute interview without first arranging to get them in. So for
a couple of days a fair amount of my time and energy was
devoted to public relations. Omitting the details, I will only
remark that it is not a good idea to persuade the *Times* that any
future item of news with your name in it will not be fit to print.

The most interesting incident Tuesday morning was my walking to a building on Thirty-fourth Street to enter a booth and
push levers on a voting machine. I have never understood why
anybody passes up that bargain. It doesn't cost a cent, and for
that couple of minutes you're the star of the show, with top
billing. It's the only way that really counts for you to say I'm it,
I'm the one that decides what's going to happen and who's going

to make it happen. It's the only time I really feel important and know I have a right to. Wonderful. Sometimes the feeling lasts all the way home if somebody doesn't bump me.

There was no sight or sound of Wolfe until he came down for lunch. No sound of the elevator, so he didn't go up to the plant rooms. I knew he was alive and breathing, because Fritz told me he cleaned up a normal breakfast, and also, when I returned from voting and a walk around a few blocks, Fritz reported that Parker had phoned and Wolfe had taken it up in his room. And the program for lunch was normal—baked bluefish stuffed with ground shrimp, and endive salad with watercress. When Wolfe came down at a quarter past one he looked in at the office door to tell me good morning, though it wasn't morning, and then crossed to the dining room. I had considered eating in the kitchen but had decided that we would have to be on speaking terms, since we had the same counsel. Also it would have given Fritz one more reason to worry, and he didn't need it.

As I got seated at the table, Wolfe asked if there had been any word from Fred or Orrie, and I said yes, they had called and I had told them to stand by, I would call them as soon as I knew what to say. He didn't mention Saul, so I assumed he had called while I was out, though Fritz hadn't said so. And he didn't mention the call from Parker. So evidently, although we were on speaking terms, the speaking wasn't going to include the matter of our right to life and liberty and the pursuit of happiness. When he had carved the bluefish and Fritz had brought me mine and taken his, he asked me where he should go to vote and I told him. Then he asked how many seats I thought the Democrats would gain in the House and the Senate, and we discussed it in detail. Then he asked if I had split the ticket, and I said yes, I had voted for Carey but not for Clark, and we discussed that.

It was quite a performance. Over the years he had had relapses and grouches, and once or twice he had come close to a tantrum, but this was a new one. Our licenses had been suspended, if we crossed the river to Jersey or drove up to Westport or Danbury we would be locked up without bail, and we had three men out on the same limb with us, but pfui. Skip it. It will all come out in the wash. And Fritz was right, he wasn't *fou,* he had merely decided that, since the situation was absolutely hopeless, he would ignore it. When we left the table at ten minutes past two, I decided to give him twenty-four hours and then issue an ultimatum, if necessary.

Four hours later I wasn't so sure. I wasn't sure of anything. When we left the dining room he had neither crossed the hall to the office nor taken the elevator back to his room; he had announced that he was going to go and vote and reached to the rack for the coat he had brought down. Certainly; voting was one of the few personal errands that got him out in any weather. But at a quarter past six he hadn't come back, and that was ridiculous. Four hours. All bets were off. He was in a hospital or the morgue, or in an airplane headed for Montenegro. I was regretting that I hadn't turned on the six-o'clock news and considering whether to start phoning now or wait until after dinner when the doorbell rang and I went to the hall, and there he was. He never carried keys. I went and opened the door and he entered, said, "I decided to do an errand," and unbuttoned his coat.

I said, "Much traffic?"

He said, "Of course. There always is."

As I hung up his coat I decided not to wait until tomorrow for the ultimatum. After dinner in the office, when Fritz had gone with the coffee tray. Wolfe went to the kitchen, and I went up to my room to stand at the window and consider how to word it.

That meal stands out as the one I enjoyed least of all the ones I have had at that table. I really thought it might be the last one, but I used my knife and fork as usual, and chewed and swallowed, and heard what he said about things like the expressions on people's faces as they stood in line in front of the voting booths. When we went to the office and sat and Fritz came with the coffee, I still hadn't decided how to start the ultimatum, but that didn't bother me. I knew from long experience that it would go better if I let it start itself.

There were a couple of swallows left of my second cup when the doorbell rang and I went for a look. It was a gang, and I went part way down the hall to make sure before I returned to the office and said, "It's four of the six. Vilar, Judd, Hahn, and Igoe. No Ackerman or Urquhart."

"None of them telephoned?"

"Yes. None."

"Bring them."

I went. I couldn't tell, as I swung the door open and they entered and got their coats off, what to expect. Evidently they hadn't come merely to deliver an ultimatum, for in the office Judd went to the red leather chair and the others moved up yellow ones. And Judd told Wolfe, "You don't look like you've just spent time in jail."

"I have spent more time in a dirtier jail," Wolfe said. "In Algiers."

"Yes? I have never been in jail. Yet. Two of us wanted to come this morning, but I wanted to get more facts. I haven't got them—not enough. Perhaps you can supply them. I understand that you and Goodwin aren't talking, not at all, and neither are the men you hired, but we are being asked about a slip of paper one of us handed Bassett at that dinner, and there has been another murder, and we are even being asked where we were Saturday morning, when that woman was killed. You said you wouldn't go to the District Attorney, and apparently you haven't. You didn't go, you were taken. We want to know what the hell is going on."

"So do I."

"Goddam it," Igoe blurted, "you'll talk to *us!*"

"I will indeed." Wolfe sent his eyes around. "I'm glad you came, gentlemen. I suppose Mr. Ackerman and Mr. Urquhart didn't want to enter this jurisdiction, and I don't blame them. As for the slip of paper, Lucile Ducos knew about it, but she was killed. Evidently Marie Garrou, the maid, also knew about it, possibly by eavesdropping, and she has talked. So you are being harassed, and that's regrettable. But I don't regret hunting you up and entangling you, because one of you supplied information that I may find useful. Two of you. Mr. Igoe told Mr. Goodwin that Mr. Bassett had obsessions—his word—and Mr. Hahn told me that one of his obsessions, a powerful one, centered on his wife."

When I heard him say that, I knew. It came in a flash, like lightning. It wasn't a guess or a hunch, I *knew*. I'm aware that you probably knew a while back and you're surprised that I didn't, but that doesn't prove that you're smarter than I am. You are just reading about it, and I was in it, right in the middle of it. Also, I may have pointed once or twice, but I'm not going back and make changes. I try to make these reports straight, straight accounts of what happened, and I'm not going to try to get tricky.

I'll try to report the rest of that conversation, but I can't swear to it. I was there and I heard it, but I had a decision to make that couldn't wait until they had gone. Obviously Wolfe was standing mute to me. Why? Damn it, *why?* But that *could* wait, and the decision couldn't. The question was, should I let him know that I now knew the score? And something happened that had happened a thousand times before: I discovered that I was only pretending to try to decide. The decision had already been made by my subconscious—I call it that because I don't know any other name for it. I was not going to let him know that I knew. If that was the way he wanted to play it, all right, it took two to play and we would see who fumbled first.

Meanwhile they were talking, and I have changed my mind. I said I would try to report the rest of that conversation, but I would be faking it. If anyone had said anything that changed the picture or added to it, I would report that, but they didn't. Wolfe tried to get Hahn and Igoe started again on Mrs. Bassett, but no. Evidently they had decided they shouldn't have mentioned her.

They had come to find out why Wolfe had dragged them in, and specifically they wanted to know—especially Judd and Vilar—about Pierre Ducos, who had died there in Wolfe's house when no one was there but us, and about his daughter. At one point I expected Wolfe to walk out on them, but he stuck and let them talk. He had admitted—stated—that it was regrettable that they were being harassed and that they had supplied useful information. Also, of course, they might possibly supply more, but they didn't. I knew they didn't, now that I had caught up.

It was a little past ten o'clock when I returned to the office after seeing them out, and I had made another decision. It would be an hour before he went up to bed, and if he started talking, it would be a job to handle my voice and my face. So instead of sitting I said, "I can catch the last half-hour of a hockey game if I hurry. Unless I'm needed?" He said no and reached for a book, and I went to the hall and reached for my coat. Outside, the wind was playing around looking for things to slap, and I turned my collar up, walked to the drugstore at the corner of Eighth Avenue, went in and to the phone booth, and dialed a number.

"Hello?"

"This is the president of the National League for Prison Reform. When would it be convenient to give me half an hour to discuss our cause?"

"Have you bathed and shaved?"

"No. I'm Exhibit A."

"All right, come ahead. Use the service entrance."

I got a break. Getting a taxi at that time of night may take anything from a minute to an hour, and here one came as I reached the curb.

Of course it was also a break that Lily was at home with no company. She had been at the piano, probably playing Chopin preludes. That isn't just a guess; I can tell by her eyes and the way she uses her voice. Her voice sounds as if it would like to sing, but she doesn't know it. She told me to go to the den and in a couple of minutes came with a tray—a bottle of champagne and two glasses.

"I put it in the freezer when you phoned," she said, "so it should be about right." She sat. "How bad was it?"

"Not bad at all. I sat on the cot and shut my eyes and pretended I was in front of the fire at The Glade with you in the kitchen broiling a steak." I pushed on the cork. "No glass for Mimi?"

"She's gone to a movie. How bad *is* it?"

"I wish I knew. I think we'll come out alive, but don't ask for odds." The cork came, and I tilted the bottle and poured. The den has a door to the terrace, and I went and opened it and stood the bottle outside. She said, "To everybody, starting with us," and we touched glasses and drank.

I sat. "Speaking of odds, if florist shops had been open I would have brought a thousand red roses. I gave you a thousand to one that Doraymee wouldn't regret telling you about Benjamin Igoe, and I'm pretty sure it was a bad bet. So I owe you an apology."

"Why will she regret it?"

"I'll tell you someday, I hope soon. I phoned and asked if I could come for three reasons. One, I like to look at you. Two, I had to apologize. Three, I thought you might be willing to answer a question or two about Doraymee."

"She doesn't like to be called that."

"All right, Dora Bassett."

"What kind of a question? Will she regret it if I answer?"

"She might. It's like this. Her husband was murdered. Your favorite waiter was murdered. His daughter was murdered. It's possible that it would help to find out who did it if you would tell me exactly what Dora Bassett said when she asked you about me. That's the question I want to ask. What did she say?"

"I told you. Didn't I?"

"Just if you had seen me since her husband died. And the second time, had I found out who put the bomb in Pierre's coat."

"Well, that was it."

"Do you remember her exact words?"

"You know darned well I don't. I'm not a tape recorder like you."

"Did she mention Nero Wolfe?"

"I think so. I'm not sure."

"Did she mention anyone else? Saul Panzer or Fred Durkin or Orrie Cather?"

"No. She was asking about you. Listen, Escamillo. I don't like this, and you know it. I told you once I don't like to think of you as a private detective, but I realize I wouldn't like to think of you as a stockbroker or a college professor or a truckdriver or a movie actor. I just like to think of you as Archie Goodwin. I like that a lot, and you know it."

She drank champagne, emptied her glass. I put down my glass, bent down to take her slipper off—blue silk or something with streaks of gold or something—poured a couple of ounces of champagne in it, lifted it to my mouth, and drank.

"That's how I like you," I said. "Hereafter I would leave my license as a detective at home if I had one. It's been suspended."

14

WHEN I went to bed and to sleep Tuesday night, I knew I was going to do something in the morning but didn't know what. I only knew that when Wolfe came down, either from the plant rooms at eleven or later for lunch, I wouldn't be there. When I opened my eyes and rolled out Wednesday morning, I knew exactly where I would be at eleven o'clock and what I would be doing. It's very convenient to have a Chairman of the Board who decides things while you sleep. At eleven o'clock I would be in the bedroom of the late Lucile Ducos, determined to find something. There *had* to be something; otherwise it might take weeks, even months.

I would have liked to go right after breakfast, but it was advisable not to tackle the white apron, now known as Marie Garrou, until she had had time to give Grandpa Ducos his breakfast and get him and his wheelchair to the window in the front room, and at least get a good start on the rest of the daily routine. So as I finished my second cup of coffee I told Fritz I would leave at tenthirty on a personal errand, and would he please tell Wolfe, who had gone up to the plant rooms, that I wouldn't be there for lunch. He asked if he should answer the phone, and I said sure, we still had our freedom of speech.

The office had been neglected for several days and needed attention. The film of dust on the chairs that hadn't been used. The stack of junk mail that had accumulated. The smell of the water in the vase on Wolfe's desk. And a dozen other details. So I didn't get away at ten-thirty. It was twenty minutes of eleven when I got ten double sawbucks from the cash box, wrote "11/6 AG 200" in the book, and closed the door of the safe. As I turned for a look around to see if I had missed anything, the doorbell rang.

It's true that there had been several pictures of her in the *Gazette* and one in the *Times,* but I assert that I would have known her anyway. It was so fit, so *natural,* for Mrs. Harvey Bassett to show, that when a woman was there on the stoop it had to be her. I had gone two miles at eleven o'clock at night to ask Lily Rowan a question about her, and there she was.

I went and opened the door and said, "Good morning," and she said, "I'm Dora Bassett. You're Archie Goodwin," and walked in and kept going, down the hall.

Any way you look at it, surely I was glad to see her, but I wasn't. For about twelve hours I had known that seeing her would certainly be on the program, but I would choose the time and place. Since Wolfe had gone up to the plant rooms, he would come down at the usual hour, and it was twelve minutes to eleven. If I followed precedent I would either go up there or go and buzz him from the kitchen, but precedent had been ignored for more than a week. So when I entered the office I didn't even glance at her—she was standing in the middle of the room—as I crossed to my desk. I sat and reached for the house phone and pushed the button.

He answered quicker than usual. "Yes?"

"Me. Mrs. Harvey H. Bassett just came. I didn't invite her. Perhaps you did."

"No." Silence. "I'll be down at once."

As I hung up she said, "I didn't come to see Nero Wolfe. I came to see you."

I looked at her. So that was Doraymee. The front of her mink or sable or sea-otter coat—it has got to the point where I can't tell cony from coonskin—was open, showing black silk or polyester. She was small but not tiny. Her face was small too, and if it hadn't been so made up, perhaps for the first time since she had lost her husband, it would probably have been easy to look at.

I stood up. "He's coming down, so you'll see both of us. I'll take your coat?"

"I want to see *you*." She tried to smile. "I know a lot about you, from your books and from Lily Rowan."

"Then you must have known Mr. Wolfe's schedule, to the office at eleven o'clock. He'll want to meet you, naturally." I moved. "I might as well take your coat."

She looked doubtful, then turned for me to get it. I put it on the couch, and when I turned she was in the red leather chair. As I went to my chair she said, "You're taller than I expected. And more—more—*rougher*. Lily thinks you're graceful."

That simply wasn't so. Lily did *not* think I was graceful. Was she trying to butter me and be subtle about it? I didn't have time to decide how to reply because the elevator had hit the bottom and I had to make sure my face was ready for Wolfe. He was not going to have the satisfaction of knowing I had caught up until I was ready.

He went to his desk and turned the chair so he would be facing her. As he sat she said, louder and stronger than before, "I came to see Archie Goodwin."

He said, just stating a fact, "This is my office, Mrs. Bassett."

"We could go to another room."

I didn't have the slightest idea of his game plan. He might have merely wanted to have a look at her and hear her voice, and intended to get up and go to the kitchen. So I told her, "I work for Mr. Wolfe, Mrs. Bassett." If it sounded sarcastic to him, fine. "I would tell him whatever you said to me. Go ahead."

She looked at me. She had fine brown eyes, really too big for her small face. Her make-up hadn't included phony lashes. "I wanted to ask you about my husband," she said. "From the newspapers and television, they seem to think his death—his—his murder—that the murder of that waiter was connected with it.

And then his daughter. And he was murdered here." She looked at Wolfe. "Here in your house."

"He was indeed," he said. "What do you want to ask about your husband?"

"Why, I just—" She cleared her throat. "It has been five days, nearly a week, and the police don't tell me anything. I thought you might. They must think you know because they arrested you because you won't talk. I thought you might tell me . . ." She fluttered a hand. "Tell me what you know."

"Then you've wasted a trip, madam. I spent two days and nights in jail rather than tell the police. I'll tell you one thing I know: the murders of your husband and that waiter *are* connected. And that woman. Of course I could tell you an assortment of lies, but I doubt if it's worth the effort. I'll tell you what I think: I think *you* could tell *me* something. It might help if you knew I wouldn't repeat it to the police. To anyone. I wouldn't. I give you my word, and my word is good."

She regarded him, her eyes straight at him. She opened her mouth and closed it again, tight. She looked at me. "Couldn't we go to another room?"

I stood up. Sometimes you don't have to make a decision, not even your subconscious; it's just there. "Certainly," I said. "My room's upstairs. Just leave your coat here."

I use the elevator about once a month, and never alone. As I took her out to it I wished there had been a mirror there on the wall so I could see Wolfe's face. In the last couple of days I had spent a lot of minutes wondering about him, and now he would spend some wondering about me. As the elevator fought its way up and we went down the hall and entered my room and I shut the door, my mind should have been on her and what line to take, but it wasn't. It was downstairs enjoying Wolfe.

But the line I would take was decided by her, not by me. As I turned from closing the door she put hands on me. First she gripped my arms, then she had her arms around my neck with her face pressed against my middle ribs, her shoulders trembling.

Well. With a woman in that position you can't even guess. She may be suggesting that you take her clothes off or she may be grabbing the nearest solid object to keep on her feet. But it seems silly just to let your arms hang, and I had mine around her, patting her back. In a minute I gave her fanny a couple of little pats, which is one way of asking a question. Her hold around my neck didn't tighten, which is one way of answering it.

Her shoulders stopped trembling. I said, "You could have done this downstairs. He would have just got up and walked out. And I could have brought you something from the kitchen. Up here there's nothing to drink but water."

She lifted her head enough to move her lips. "I don't want a drink. I wanted *this*. I want your arms around me."

"You do not. You just want arms around you, not necessarily mine. Not that I mind pinch-hitting. Come and sit down."

Her arms loosened. I patted her back again, then put my hands up and around and got her wrists. She let go and straightened up and even used a hand to brush her hair back from her eyes and adjust the fur thing that was perched on it. There were two chairs, a big easy one over by the reading lamp and a small straight one at the little desk. I steered her across to the big one and went and brought the small one.

She had come guessing and she would have to leave guessing. Of course I would have liked to know a lot of things that she knew, and her arms around my neck with her shoulders shaking showed that I could probably pry them out of her, but if I tried to, she would have known how much *I* knew, and that wouldn't do. Not yet. So as I sat I said, "I'm sorry that's all I have for you, Mrs. Bassett, just a pair of arms. If you thought I could tell you something that the police don't know or won't tell, I can't. We aren't talking to the police because we have nothing to say. If you have read some of my books, you must know that Nero Wolfe is one of a kind. I admit I'm a little curious about you. Miss Rowan told me you never read books. Why have you read some of mine?"

From the way her big brown eyes looked at me, you wouldn't have thought she had just had her arms around my neck. Nor from her tone as she asked, "What else did she tell you about me?"

"Nothing much. She just mentioned that she had seen you and you had asked her about me."

"I asked her about you because I knew she knew you and your picture was in the paper."

"Sure. Yours was too. Why did you read some of my books?"

"I didn't. I told her I did because I knew about her and you." She stood up. "I'm sorry I came. I guess I—I just thought . . ." She shook her head. "I don't know what I thought. I don't want— My coat's in there where he is."

I was up. I told her I would get her coat and went and opened the door, and she came. That elevator is one of a kind too; it complains more about going down than about going up. Downstairs, she stayed in the hall when I went into the office for her coat. Wolfe wasn't there; presumably he had gone to the kitchen. I wrote on a sheet of my memo pad:

NW:
I'm taking Mrs. B. home. Probably not back for lunch.

                                 AG

I put it under a paperweight on his desk, went to the hall with Mrs. Bassett's mink or sable or sea otter and held it for her, put my coat on, and let us out. Her Rolls-Royce was there at the curb, but I didn't go and open the door for her because as we descended to the sidewalk the chauffeur climbed out and had it open by the time she was down. When he got back in and it rolled, I walked to Ninth Avenue and turned uptown.

It was ten minutes past noon when I pushed the button in the vestibule at 318 West Fifty-fourth Street. Three minutes passed with no response, and I shook my head. They might have cleared out. It had been four days since the daughter had been killed; the old man might be in a hospital. They might even have gone back to France. But then her voice came, exactly as before: "Who ees eet?"

"Archie Goodwin, from Nero Wolfe. I don't want to bother Mr. Ducos, and anyway I don't speak French, as you know. I'd like to come up, if you can spare a few minutes."

"What for? I don't know anything."

"Maybe not, but Nero Wolfe and I would appreciate it. Sill voo play."

"You don't speak French."

"I know I don't, but everybody knows those three words, even dummies like me. Please?"

"Well . . . for Nero Wolfe . . ."

The click sounded, and I pushed the door and was in, and the elevator was there with the door open. Upstairs, the door of the apartment was open too and she was there on the sill, white apron and cap exactly as before. She looked even shorter and dumpier, and the crease in the double chin looked deeper. From the way she stood and the expression on her face, it was obvious I wasn't going to be invited in, so I had to try throwing a punch, hoping it would land.

"I suppose I call you Marie," I said.

She nodded. "That's my name." You'll have to supply her accent; I'm not going to try to spell it.

"Well, Marie, you probably prefer straight talk, so I'll just say that I know you heard Miss Ducos and me talk that evening. You must have. You told the police about the slip of paper, and other things. Or you may have heard Mr. Ducos and Nero Wolfe talking. I'm not saying you listened when you shouldn't, I'm just saying that you heard. I don't know if you heard Miss Ducos tell me that you didn't like her. Did you?"

"I don't listen when I shouldn't listen."

"I didn't say you do. But you must know *she* didn't like *you*. A woman knows when another woman doesn't like her."

"She's dead, but it won't hurt her to say I didn't like her. I didn't hate her, I had no reason to hate her. And she's dead. You didn't come just to tell me I didn't like her."

"No. It's warm in here." I took my coat off. "I came because we think there's something here that will help us find the man who killed Pierre. Probably the slip of paper, but it could be something else. That's what I was looking for in Pierre's room. But I didn't find it, and maybe it wasn't there, maybe it was in her room, and of course she knew it was. Maybe it's still there, and that's what I came for, to see if I can find it."

No visible reaction. She just said, "The police looked in her room."

"Of course, naturally they would, but they probably weren't very thorough. Anyway, they didn't find it, so I would like to try. Nero Wolfe could have come to ask Mr. Ducos to let me look, but he didn't want to bother him. You can stay with me to see that I don't do anything I shouldn't do."

She was shaking her head. "No." She repeated it. "No."

There are a thousand ways of saying no and I had heard a lot of them. Sometimes it's more the eyes than the tone of voice that tells you what kind of a no it is. Her little dark eyes, nearly black, were a little too close together, and they blinked a little too often. It was ten to one that I couldn't sell her, but even money, maybe better, that I could buy her. "Look, Marie," I said, "you know a man gave Pierre a hundred dollars for that slip of paper."

"No. A hundred dollars? I don't know that."

"Well, he did. But Pierre might have made a copy of it. And Lucile might have found it and made a copy too." My hand went to my pocket and came out with the little roll I had taken from the cash box. I draped my coat over my arm to have both hands and peeled off five of the ten twenties and returned them to my pocket. "All right," I said, "I'll give *you* a hundred dollars to give me a chance to find Lucile's copy or to find something else that may be in her room. It may take five minutes or it may take five hours. Here, take it."

Her eyes said she would, but her hands didn't move. The

white apron had two little pockets, and I folded the bills into a little wad and stuck it in her left pocket, and said, "If you don't want to stay with me, you can search me before I leave."

"Only *her* room," she said.

"Right," I said, and she backed up, and I entered. She turned, and I followed her down the hall to Lucile's room. She entered but went in only a couple of steps, and I crossed to a chair by a window and put my coat on it.

"I'm not going to stay," she said. "I have things to do, and you're Archie Goodwin, and I told you, I know about you and Nero Wolfe from him. Do you want a cup of coffee?"

I said no thanks, and she left.

If it was a slip of paper, the most likely place was the books, but after seeing me doing her father's room she might have put it somewhere else. There was a desk with drawers by the right wall, and I went and opened the top drawer. It was locked, but the key was sticking in the lock, probably left there by a city employee. It held an assortment—several kinds of notepaper and envelopes, stubs of bills, presumably paid bills, pencils and pens, a bunch of snapshots with a rubber band around them. Five minutes was enough for that. The second drawer was full of letters in envelopes addressed to Miss Lucile Ducos, various sizes and shapes and colors. A collection of letters is always a problem. If you don't read them, the feeling that you may have missed a bus nags you, and if you do read them it's a hundred to one that there won't be a damn thing you can use. I was taking one out of the envelope just for a look when a bell rang somewhere, not in that room. Not the telephone, probably the doorbell, and I made a face. It probably wasn't a Homicide man, since the murder was four days old, but it could be, and I cocked my ear and heard Marie's voice, so faint I didn't get the words. The voice stopped, and there were footsteps.

She appeared at the door. "A man down there says his name is Sole Panzaire and Nero Wolfe sent him. He wants to come up."

"Did you tell him I'm here?"

"Yes."

"You told him my name?"

"Yes."

"I guess Nero Wolfe sent him to help me." I got the rest of the bills from my pocket and crossed over to her. "He does that sometimes without telling me." Her apron pocket was empty, and I folded one of the twenties and reached to put it in. "Saul Panzer is a good man, Nero Wolfe trusts him. With him to help, it won't take so long."

"I don't like it."

"We don't like it either, Marie, but we want to find the man that killed Pierre."

She turned and went. I started to follow her, decided not to, went back to the desk, listened for the sound of the elevator, and didn't hear it until it stopped on that floor. I opened the drawer and was taking a letter from an envelope when there were footsteps and then Saul's voice. "Any luck, Archie?"

He would. Saving his surprise until there were no other ears to hear it. "Don't push," I told him. "I just got started." I walked to the door for a look in the hall. Empty. I shut the door. He was putting his coat on the chair with mine. "So that's where he was yesterday afternoon," I said. "He went to see you. I'll try not to get in your way, but I'm not going to leave."

We were face to face, eye to eye. "You're on," he said.

"You're damn right I'm on. I'm on my own."

He laughed. Not with his mouth, no noise; he laughed with his eyes, and by shaking his head. And he didn't stop. "Laugh your goddam head off," I said, "but don't get in *my* way. I'm busy." I went to the desk and reached to the drawer for a letter, and my hand was trembling. Saul's voice came from behind.

"Archie, this is the first time I ever knew you to miss one completely. I supposed you had it figured and was enjoying it. You actually didn't know that he thought you'd kill him? That he thinks he *knows* you would?"

The letter dropped from my hand, and I guess my mouth dropped open as I turned. "Balls," I said.

"But he does. He says you wouldn't do it with a gun or a club, just with your hands. You'd hit him so hard you'd break his neck, or you'd throw him so hard and so far he'd break his neck when he landed. I didn't try to argue him out of it, because he *knew* it."

"I thought he knew me. And you think it's funny."

"I *know* it's funny. He does know you. I thought you knew him. It's just that he wants to kill him himself. So do I. So do you."

"Were you on?"

"Not till he came yesterday, but I should have been. A lot of things—Pierre not telling you, that room at Rusterman's, her asking Lily Rowan about you, him and women, him offering to work for nothing, him wanting to take Lucile Ducos—I certainly should have been on." He tapped his skull with his knuckles. "Empty."

"Mine too, until last night. Have you got anything?"

"Nothing solid. I only started to look yesterday at half past five. I've got an idea how he might have met her. As you know, he often does jobs for Del Bascom, and Bascom took on something for Bassett, for NATELEC, about a year ago. At noon I decided to take a look here, and here you are ahead of me."

"Not much ahead, I just started. Okay. I came for myself, and you came for him. Who's in charge?"

He grinned. "It's a temptation, sure it is, but I'm not like Oscar Wilde, I can resist it. Where do you want me to start?"

I was returning the grin. Saul doesn't often drag in such facts as that he knows about people like Oscar Wilde and I don't. "You might try this desk," I said. "I've only done the top drawer. There's a lot of books, and I'll start on them."

15

TWO HOURS LATER, when Marie came, we had covered a lot of ground, at least Saul had, and had found exactly nothing. He had done the desk, chairs, closet, bed, floor, dresser, pictures on the wall, and a stack of magazines, and had really done them. Flipping through the hundred and some books had taken me half an hour, and then I had settled down to it, starting over and turning the pages one by one, making sure not to skip. Saul was having another go at shoes from the closet, examining the insides, when the door opened and Marie was there with a loaded tray. She crossed to the table and put the tray down and said, "I went out for the beer. We only drink mineral water. I hope you like *fromage de cochon*. Monsieur Ducos makes it himself. His chair won't go in the kitchen, and I put things in the hall for him."

I had joined her. "Thank you very much," I said. "I admit I'm hungry. *Thank* you." My hand came out of my pocket, but she showed me a palm. "No," she said, "you are guests"—and walked out.

There was a plate with a dozen slices of something, a long, slender loaf of bread, and the beer. Of course Pierre had told her that Nero Wolfe liked beer, and we were from Nero Wolfe, so she went out for beer. I would remember to tell him. We moved the table over by the bed, and I sat on the bed and Saul on the chair. There was no bread knife. Of course; you yank it off. No butter. The slices, *fromage de cochon,* which I looked up a week later, was head cheese, and I hope Fritz doesn't read this, because I'm going to state a fact: it was better than his. We agreed that it was the best head cheese we had ever tasted, and the bread was good enough to go with it. I told Saul I was glad we were getting something for the six double sawbucks I had given her.

Half an hour later it was looking as though that was all we were going to get. We looked at each other, and Saul said, "I skipped something. I didn't look close enough at the inside of the covers. Did you?" I said maybe not, and we each took a book, he from the top shelf and I from the middle one, and the third book I took, there it was. *The Feminine Mystique* by Betty Friedan. The inside of the back cover was pasted-on paper like all books, but it bulged a little in the middle and at the outside edge the edge of another paper showed, about a sixty-fourth of an inch. I got out my knife and opened the small thin blade. Saul put his book back on the shelf and said, "Easy does it," and I didn't even glance at him, which showed the condition we were in. We never say things like that to each other.

I went easy all right. It took a good five minutes to make sure that it was glued down tight except for a small part in the middle, a rectangle about one inch by an inch and a half, where the little bulge was. Then came the delicate part, getting under to the edge of whatever made the bulge. That took another five minutes, but once I had the edge it was simple. I slit along to the corner, then across the end and down the other side, and across the other end. And there it was. A piece of thin paper glued to the paper that had bulged, with writing on it in ink. I am looking at it right now, and the other day I took a picture of it with my best camera to reproduce here:

Orrie Cather
127 E. 94

I handed it to Saul, and he took a look and handed it back and said, "She wrote it."

"Sure. The one Pierre found on the tray, Orrie gave him a hundred dollars for it. That was four days after the dinner, so Pierre had it four days. I said a week ago that she found it and made a copy of it, and she would try to put the squeeze on him and would get killed. ESP." I got out my card case and slipped the piece of paper in under cellophane.

I stood up. "Have you got a program? I have. I'm not going to report in person. I'm going to the nearest phone booth."

"I don't suppose I could listen in?"

"Sure, why not?"

We took a look around. Everything was in order except the table, which was still by the bed, and we put it back where it belonged. Saul took our coats and the book, and I took the tray. We found Marie in the kitchen, which was about one-fourth the size of Wolfe's. I told her the bread and wonderful head cheese had saved our lives, that we hadn't found what we had hoped to find, and that we were taking just one thing, a book that we wanted to have a good look at because it might tell us something. She wouldn't let me pay for the book, because Miss Ducos was dead and they didn't want it. She declined my offer to let her go through our pockets and came to the door to let us out. All in all, we had got my money's worth.

Out on the sidewalk I told Saul, "I said the nearest phone booth, but if you listen in it will be crowded. How about your place?" He said fine, and that his car was parked in the lot near Tenth Avenue, and we headed west. He doesn't like to talk when he's driving any more than I do, but he'll listen, and I told him about the uninvited guest who had come that morning, and he said he wished he had been there, he would have liked to have a look at her.

We left the car in the garage on Thirty-ninth Street where he keeps it and walked a couple of blocks. He lives alone on the top floor of a remodeled house on Thirty-eighth Street between Lexington and Third. The living room is big, lighted with two floor lamps and two table lamps. One wall had windows, one was solid with books, and the other two had doors to the closet and hall, and pictures, and shelves that were cluttered with everything from chunks of minerals to walrus tusks. In the far corner was a grand piano. The telephone was on a desk between windows. He was the only operative in New York who asked and got twenty dollars an hour that year, and he had uses for it.

When I sat at the desk and started to dial, he left for the bedroom, where there's an extension. It was a quarter past four, so Wolfe would be down from the plant rooms. Fritz might answer, or he might; it depended on what he was doing.

"Yes?" Him.

"Me. I have a detailed report. I'm with Saul at his place. I didn't take Mrs. Bassett home. At a quarter past twelve I started to search the room of Lucile Ducos. At half past, Saul came and offered to help me. Marie Garrou brought us a plate of marvelous head cheese, for which I paid her a hundred and twenty dollars. I mention that so you won't have to ask if I have eaten. At half past three we found a slip of paper which Lucile had hidden in a book, on which she had written Orrie's name and address. I knew it was Orrie last night when you mentioned what Hahn and Igoe had said about Bassett's obsession on his wife. Saul says you thought I would kill him—that you *knew* I would. Nuts. You may be a genius, but nuts. I once looked genius up in that book of quotations. Somebody said that all geniuses have got a touch of madness. Apparently yours—"

"Seneca."

"Apparently your touch of madness picks on me. That will have to be discussed someday. Now there is a problem, and finding that slip of paper in one of her books—it was *The Feminine Mystique* by Betty Friedan, and I've got it—that settles it, and Saul won't have to do any more digging. As I said, I'm at his place. Fred will be expecting word from you; he won't be working. We're going to have him come, and we'll decide what to do, us three. I have an idea, but we'll discuss it. As far as I'm concerned, you're out of it. You told us your emotions had taken over on Nixon and Watergate, and they have certainly taken over on this—what you thought you knew about me. So. I won't hang up; I'll listen if you want to talk."

He hung up.

I went to the piano and spread my fingers to hit a chord that shows you've decided something, according to Lily. When I turned, Saul was standing there. He didn't say anything, just stood with his brows raised.

I spoke. "I was just following instructions. He instructed us to ignore his decisions and instructions."

"That's a funny sentence."

"I feel funny."

"So do I. Do you want to call Fred, or shall I?"

I said that since Fred was being invited to his place, I thought he should, and he went to the desk and dialed, and didn't have to wait for an answer. Fred must have been sticking near the phone. He would; he hates unfinished business more than either of us.

Saul hung up. "He's on his way. Half an hour, maybe less. Milk or bourbon or what?"

"Nothing, thanks, not right now. You heard me say I have an idea, but I need to take a good look at it before I share it. It's one hell of a problem. Have you got a script?"

"No. Not even a first draft. I want to give it a look too."

Daylight was about gone, and he went and turned on lights and pulled the window drapes. I went and sat on a chair at the table where we played poker. It was by far the worst mess I had ever looked at. If you went at it from one angle, some other angle tripped you up and you had to go back and start over. For instance, Jill, the airline hostess Orrie had married a few years ago when he had decided to settle down and quit trying to prove that Casanova had been a piker, as Saul had once put it. She still had a strong hold on him, and since she was now going to get a hell of a jolt, no matter how we handled it, why not use her? For another instance, Dora Bassett. I didn't know how she felt about him now, but we could find out, and maybe we could use *her*. And three or four other angles. With any and all of them, of course the bottom question was could we possibly come out with a whole skin, all four of us? It was only when the doorbell rang and Saul went to let Fred in that I realized that I had just been shadow-boxing. No matter how we played it, one thing *had* to happen, and the surest and quickest way to that had to come first.

Saul, always a good host, had a couple of chairs in place in front of the couch and liquids on the coffee table—Ten Mile bourbon for Fred and me and brandy for him—and we sat and poured, Fred on the couch.

"I said on the phone," Saul told Fred, "that it's a powwow. Actually it's a council of war. Tell him, Archie."

"You tell him. You knew before I did."

"Only because Mr. Wolfe told me. But all right. Fred, Orrie Cather killed all three of them."

Fred nodded. "I know he did."

Saul stared at him and said, "What?" I stared and said, "That's the first time I ever heard you tell a double-breasted lie."

"It's not a lie, Archie. I knew it when he asked Mr. Wolfe to give him Lucile Ducos instead of Saul. Why didn't he know Mr. Wolfe wouldn't? That was crazy. Of course there was another thing too, he knew all about that room at Rusterman's. But it was his asking to take Lucile Ducos. That was absolutely cockeyed. Of course I knew I was wrong because Mr. Wolfe didn't know."

"I pass," Saul said. "I'm with Alice in Wonderland. First Archie follows instructions by ignoring instructions, and now you knew it was Orrie but you knew you were wrong."

"I pass too," I said. "All of you knew before I did. I'm out of my class. You talk, and I'll listen."

"You had a hurdle we didn't have," Saul said. "You knew Orrie wanted your job and thought he might get it. You've always gone easy on him, made allowances for him that Fred or I wouldn't make. It's in your reports. You had blinders that we didn't. *I* should have known. You said you had an idea and wanted to give it a good look, and the blinders are off now. Let's have it."

I took a sip of bourbon and a swallow of water. "I just *thought* I had an idea. I was just slashing around. Actually all I've got is facts. Two facts. One, Orrie has asked for it and has to get it. He has bought it, and it has to be delivered. Two, Nero Wolfe, the great detective, the genius, is hogtied. He can't make a move. If he goes by the book, collects the pieces and hands Cramer the package, he will have to get on the witness stand and answer questions under oath about a man he has used and trusted for years. He wouldn't do that, he would rather spend ten years behind bars than do that. You know damn well he wouldn't, and I'm glad he wouldn't. All of us would have to answer questions in public about a guy we have worked with and played pinochle with."

I swallowed bourbon, too big a swallow, and had to swallow air for a chaser. "I don't think he could stand the sight of Orrie Cather. That's why we had to meet here instead of at the office. An hour ago on the telephone I told him we were going to get Fred and decide what to do, and I asked him if he wanted to talk, and he hung up. If we walked into the office with Orrie, he would walk out. He couldn't take it. So we—"

"I'll tell you something," Fred said. "I don't think I could take it either. If he walked in here right now, I wouldn't walk out, I would kill him. I've got my gun, I always carry a gun at night now, but I wouldn't shoot him, I'd break his neck."

"We would all like to break his neck," Saul said, "but we've got necks too. Of course he has to get it, and it's up to us to deliver it, the question is how." He looked at me. "I thought that was the idea you wanted to look at."

I nodded. "We'll all look at it." I looked at my watch: 5:22.

"I suggest that you ring him and invite him to come at nine o'clock. Just for a powwow. Okay, Fred?"

He lifted his glass, looked at it, and put it down. "I guess so. Hell, we have to, don't we?"

Saul got up and went to the desk and picked up the phone.

16

I WOULDN'T WANT to go through that again. I don't mean the three hours while we discussed it and decided what to do. The hour after he came, while we did it.

I'm not even sure we would have gone through with it if it hadn't been for the bomb. We felt silly, at least I did, standing there at the door of the apartment while he was on his way up the three flights, standing so he could only see Saul as he approached —Saul in the doorway to greet the arriving guest.

As I think I mentioned, Orrie was half an inch taller than me and fully as broad, without a flabby ounce on him. As he stepped in, we jumped him, Saul from the back and Fred and I from the sides, and pinned him. His reflex, his muscles acting on their own, lasted only half a second. Saul's arm was around his neck, locking him. No one said anything. Saul started to go over him from behind, first his right side and then his left. His topcoat wasn't buttoned. From under his left arm Saul took his gun, which was of course to be expected, and dropped it on the rug. Then from his inside breast pocket Saul's hand came out with something that was not to be expected because Orrie didn't smoke: an aluminum cigar tube. Don Pedro.

Fred said, "Jesus Christ."

As I said, without that I'm not sure we would have gone through with it. Saul made sure the cap was screwed on tight and put it in his own breast pocket and finished the frisking job. Fred and I turned loose and moved back, and Orrie turned and took a step. Going to leave. Actually. Saul was there and kicked the door shut. I said, "Hell, you might have known, Orrie. You *should* have known. Coming here with that in your pocket? What do you take us for?"

Fred said, "*You* said it, Saul. You said we had to jump him. Jesus Christ."

Saul said, "On in, Orrie. It's our deal."

I had never had the idea that Orrie Cather was dumb. He was no Saul Panzer, but he wasn't dumb. But he was dumb then. "What for?" he said. "All right, you've got it." His voice was almost normal, just squeezed a little. "I'm not going to blow. I'm going home."

"Oh, no, you're not," Fred said. "My god, don't you know it's coming and you've got to take it?"

Saul had picked up the gun, an old S & W .38 Orrie had had for years, and stuck it in his pocket. "On in, Orrie. Move. We're going to talk." I took hold of his left arm. He jerked loose and took a step and kept going, to the arch and on into the big room. Saul got ahead of him and led the way across to the couch. The four of us had played pinochle in that room. We had tagged Paul Rago for murder in that room. Orrie took the chair in the middle, with Saul on his left and Fred on his right, and me on the couch. As Saul sat, he said, "Tell him, Archie."

"Fred has already told you," I told Orrie. "You've got to take it. We're not going to turn you in. I don't have to explain why that wouldn't—"

"You don't have to explain anything."

"Then I won't. I'll just tell you what we're going to do. We're going to make it impossible for you to live. I'm going to see Jill tomorrow, or Saul is. You're through with her. You're through with any kind of work, not only in New York. Anywhere in the world. You're through with any kind of contact with people that means anything. You know us and you know Nero Wolfe. We know what it will cost us, Nero Wolfe in money and us in time and effort, but that's what we have to pay for not realizing long ago that someday, somehow, we would be sorry we didn't cross you off. Exactly how—"

"You didn't have any reason to cross me off."

"Certainly we did. For instance, Isabel Kerr. Eight years ago. You got yourself in the can on a murder rap, and it was a job to get you out. And—"

"That was just a bad break. You know damn well it was."

"Skip it. It isn't just a bad break that you have killed three people. It isn't just—"

"You can't prove it. You can't prove a damned thing."

Fred said, "Jesus Christ." I said, "We don't have to prove it. We don't want to prove it. I told you, we're not going to turn you in, we're going to make it impossible for you to live. You've bought it, and we're going to deliver it. Actually, we *could* prove it, but you know what it would mean, especially for Nero Wolfe. We could probably prove the first one, Bassett. As you know, they have got the bullet that killed him, a thirty-eight, and the gun that fired it is probably now in Saul's pocket. And Pierre—"

"That was self-defense, Archie. Bassett was going to ruin me."

"Pierre wasn't going to ruin you."

"Yes, he was. When he learned about Bassett he remembered about me and the slip of paper. I had been damn fool enough to give him a hundred dollars for the slip of paper. He demanded a thousand dollars. A grand. He came that Sunday, two days after Bassett, and asked for a grand. He said that was all he wanted, he wouldn't come back, but you know how that is. You said once that all blackmailers ought to be shot."

"You didn't shoot him. Sunday? The next day or evening you went to that room at Rusterman's and put that thing in his coat pocket. Then his daughter was going to ruin you, and you shot her, and they've got that bullet too. You had another bomb, probably got two for the price of one, but you couldn't use it on her because she knew what had killed her father. And you brought it with you here tonight. I thought Saul did a good job with his voice on the phone, but I suppose after killing three people your nerves are on edge. And we *are* going to ruin you."

Saul got up and left the room. Sometimes a trip to the bathroom can't be postponed. But it wasn't the bathroom; his footsteps on the tiled hall floor went on to the kitchen. Fred rose and stretched his legs and sat down again. Orrie glanced up at him and then sent his eyes back to me. No one spoke. Footsteps again, and Saul was back. Instead of returning to his chair, he joined me and on the couch between us he put what he had gone for: a roll of adhesive tape, a pair of pliers, and a couple of paper towels. He got the Don Pedro cigar tube from his pocket, checked the cap again, gripped it in the middle with the pliers, wiped it good with a paper towel, laid it on the edge of the other paper towel, and rolled the towel around it, tucking in the ends. Then about a yard of adhesive tape, all the way with both ends covered. A very neat wrapping job, with an appreciative audience.

"We'll keep the gun," he said. "As you said, Archie, we're not going to turn him in, but we'll keep it just in case. But he can have this. Right?"

"Sure," I said. "Now that you've gift-wrapped it. Fred?"

"I guess so." Fred nodded. "Okay."

Saul got up and offered it, but Orrie didn't take it. His hands were on his knees, the curled fingers moving in and out a little as if they couldn't decide whether to make fists. He hadn't taken his topcoat off. Saul stepped to him, pulled open his topcoat and jacket, put the tube back where he had found it, in the inside breast pocket, and went to his chair. Orrie's hand went into the pocket and came out again, empty.

"Dora Bassett came to see us this morning," I told Orrie. "I took her up to my room, and we had a talk. I'll see Jill tomorrow, if she's not on a flight."

"I'll go along," Fred said. "I like Jill."

"I'll start with Del Bascom," Saul said. "Then Pete Vawter."

Orrie stood up and said, "I'm going to see Nero Wolfe."

We all stared at him. Fred said, "Jesus Christ." Saul said, "How are you going to get in?" I said, "He won't. Of course not. He's cracked."

Orrie turned and walked out. Saul got up and followed, and I tagged along, and Fred was right behind me. My mind was on a point of etiquette—should you open the door for a departing guest in whose pocket you have just put a bomb that you hope he'll use? Saul didn't; he stayed behind. Orrie not only opened the door, he pulled it shut after him, with us standing there. The spring lock clicked in place, but Saul slid the bolt, which was sensible. Orrie was good with locks, and he just might have ideas. Apparently no one felt like talking; we stood there.

"No bets," I said. "No bets either way."

"Me neither," Saul said. "Not a dime. If it takes a year, it will be a bad year for all of us. And you have a family, Fred."

"Right here and now," Fred said, "I've got me, and I'm empty. I could swallow some of that salami I turned down, if you can spare it."

"*That's* a bet," Saul said and headed for the kitchen.

17

AT A QUARTER PAST ELEVEN Thursday morning I pushed the button at the door of the old brownstone for Fritz to come and slide the bolt. Behind my elbows were Saul and Fred. Fred had gone home to his own bed and come back at nine o'clock, but I had slept on the couch in Saul's living room. I hadn't overslept, and neither had Saul; we had turned on the radio at six and seven and eight and nine and ten, so we were well informed on current events. A little after ten I had called the *Gazette* and left word for Lon Cohen that I could be reached at Saul's place until eleven and then at the office. I hadn't called Wolfe. I had told him we were going to decide what to do, and let him think we were spending the night at it. For breakfast Saul and I had had two thick slices of broiled ham, six poached eggs, and about a dozen thin slices of buttered toast sprinkled with chives. Saul grows chives in a sixteen-inch box in his kitchen window.

It wouldn't be accurate reporting to say that Wolfe's mouth dropped open when he saw us walk in, but it might have, though it never had, if he hadn't heard our voices in the hall. What he did do, he put on an act. He finished a paragraph in a book he was reading, took his time inserting the thin strip of gold he used for a bookmark, put the book down, and said, "Good morning."

Saul went to the red leather chair, Fred pulled up a yellow one, and I went to my desk, sat, and said, "I have asked Saul to report. He was the host."

Saul said, "Fred came about an hour after Archie phoned you. I called Orrie and asked him to come at nine o'clock. We decided to try to make him kill himself. When he came we jumped him without warning. He had his gun as usual, and in a pocket of his jacket he had a Don Pedro cigar tube. We went in and sat down and talked for about half an hour. Mostly Archie talked. He told him we were going to make it impossible for him to live. Orrie said Bassett was going to ruin him and Pierre hit him for a thousand dollars. I sealed the cigar tube with adhesive tape and put it back in his pocket, but we kept his gun. He left a little before ten o'clock."

Wolfe said, "Satisfactory," but he said it only with his eyes. His mouth stayed shut tight. He leaned back and closed his eyes and breathed deep. Saul looked at me and was going to say something, but he didn't get it out because he was interrupted by a noise. Two noises. First the ring of the doorbell, and a moment later a shattering crack and clatter, somewhere close. We jumped and ran to the hall, Fred in front because he was closest. But in the hall he stopped and I passed him. As I neared the front door I slowed because the floor was covered with pieces of glass. There was nothing left of the glass panel in the door, three feet by four feet, but some jagged edges. I slid the bolt and opened the door enough to get through and stepped out.

Down on the sidewalk at the foot of the steps was Orrie Cather's topcoat. From up above that's just what it was, his top-coat. I went down the seven steps, and then I could see his face. There was nothing much wrong with his face. He had liked his face too much to hold it the way Pierre had held it. Nine days and ten hours had passed, two hundred and twenty-six hours, since I had stood and looked down at what had been Pierre's face.

I lifted my head, and Saul and Fred were there, one on each side. "Okay," I said, "stand by. I'm going in and ring Lon Cohen. I owe him something."

18

AT HALF PAST NINE that evening Wolfe and I were leaving the dining room, an hour later than usual, for after-dinner coffee in the office, when the doorbell rang. Wolfe shot a glance at the front door. He didn't stop, but he had seen who it was, because I had stood my ground with Ralph Kerner of Town House Services and insisted that the temporary emergency job on the front door had to include some one-way glass. The bolt was a new one and wasn't well fitted. I slid it and opened up, and Inspector Cramer entered.

He gave me a funny look, as if he wanted to ask me a question but couldn't decide how to put it. Then he looked around, at the marks on the wall and bench and rack, and the floor mat. I said, "The glass. You should have seen it." He said, "Yeah, I bet," and headed down the hall. I followed.

He always goes straight to the red leather chair, but not that time. Three steps in he stopped and sent his eyes around, left to right and then right to left. Then he went to the big globe and turned it, in no hurry, clear around, first to the right and then to the left, while I stood and stared. Then he took off his coat and dropped it on a yellow chair, crossed to the red leather chair, sat, and said, "I've been wanting to do that for years. I don't think I've ever mentioned that it's the biggest and finest globe I ever saw. Also I've never mentioned that this is the best working room I know. The best-looking. I mention it now because I may never see it again."

"Indeed." Wolfe's brows were up. "Are you retiring? You're not old enough."

"No, I'm not retiring. Maybe I should. I'm not old enough, but I'm tired enough. But I'm not. But you are. You could call it retiring."

"Apparently you have been misinformed. Or are you guessing?"

"No, I'm not guessing." Cramer got a cigar from a pocket, not a Don Pedro, stuck it in his mouth and clamped his teeth on it, and took it out again. He hadn't lit one for years. "It's no go, Wolfe. This time you *are* done. Not only the DA, the Commissioner. I think he has even spoken to the Mayor. Is this being recorded?"

"Of course not. My word of honor if you need it."

"I don't." Cramer put the cigar between his teeth, took it out, threw it at my wastebasket, and missed by two feet. "You know," he said, "I don't really know how dumb you think I am. I never have known."

"Pfui. That's flummery. My knowledge of you is not mere surmise. I *know* you. Certainly your mental processes have limits, so have mine, but you are not dumb—your word—at all. If you were dumb, you would have in fact concluded that I am done—again, your word—and you wouldn't have come. You would have abandoned me to the vengeance of the District Attorney—perhaps with a touch of regret that you wouldn't have another chance to come and whirl that globe around."

"Goddam it, I didn't *whirl* it!"

"Spin, rotate, twirl, circumvolute—your choice. So why did you come?"

"*You* tell *me.*"

"I will. Because you suspected that I might not be done, there might be a hole I could wriggle out through, and you wanted to know where and how."

"That would be a wriggle. You wriggle?"

"Confound it, quit scorning my diction. I choose words to

serve my purpose. Archie, tell Fritz he may bring the coffee. Three cups. Or would you prefer beer or brandy?"

Cramer said no, he would like coffee, and I went. Tired as I was after a long, hard day, including such items as telling Jill what had happened to Orrie, I didn't drag my feet. I too wanted to know where and how. When I went back in, Wolfe was talking.

". . . but I'm not going to tell you what I intend to do. Actually I don't intend to do anything. I'm going to loaf, drift, for the first time in ten days. Read books, drink beer, discuss food with Fritz, logomachize with Archie. Perhaps chat with you if you have occasion to drop in. I'm loose, Mr. Cramer. I'm at peace."

"Like hell you are. Your licenses have been suspended."

"Not for long, I think. When the coffee comes—"

It came. Fritz was there with the tray. He put it on Wolfe's desk and left. Wolfe poured, and he remembered that Cramer took sugar and cream, though it had been at least three years since he had had coffee with us. I got up and served Cramer and got mine, sat and stirred and took a sip, and crossed my legs, hoping that by bedtime I would be at peace too.

Wolfe took a swallow—he can take coffee hotter than I can—and leaned back. "I told you nine days ago," he said, "Tuesday of last week, that I was going to tell you absolutely nothing. I repeat that. I am going to tell you nothing. But if you care to listen, I'll make a supposition. I'll imagine a situation and describe it. Do you want me to?"

"You can start. I can always interrupt." Cramer took too big a sip of hot coffee. I was afraid he would have to spit it out, but his mouth and jaw worked on it and he got it down.

"A long and elaborate supposition," Wolfe said. "Suppose that five days ago, last Saturday, an accumulation of facts and observations forced me to surmise that a man who had been associated with me for years had committed three murders. The first item of that accumulation had come the morning Pierre Ducos died in my house when Archie—I drop the formality—

Archie told me what Pierre had said when he arrived. He refused to give Archie any details; he would tell only me. Perhaps it was my self-esteem that made me give that item too little thought; Pierre said I was the greatest detective in the world. All is vanity."

He drank coffee. "The second item of the accumulation came Wednesday evening, a week ago yesterday, when Orrie Cather offered to donate his services, to take no pay. He made the offer first, before either Saul Panzer or Fred Durkin. That was out of character. For him it was remarkable. Shall I iterate and reiterate that this is merely a series of suppositions?"

"Hell no. You're just imagining it. Sure. Go ahead."

"The third item was an old fact. The best opportunity—the only one I knew of—for someone to put the bomb in Pierre's pocket had been when he was at work and his coat was in his locker at the restaurant. Orrie Cather was familiar with that room; he had once helped with an investigation there, and the lock would have been no problem for him. The fourth item was that Mrs. Harvey Bassett questioned a friend of hers about Archie Goodwin—had she seen him, and had he learned who had killed Pierre Ducos. The fifth item was that Mr. Bassett had an obsession about his wife—information supplied by two of the men who were at that dinner. It was at that point that I first thought it possible that Orrie Cather was somehow involved, for the sixth item was my knowledge of Orrie's contacts with women and his habitual conduct with them."

He emptied his cup and poured, and I took Cramer's cup and mine and got refills.

"As I said," Wolfe resumed, "it's a long and elaborate supposition. The seventh item was another mention of Mrs. Bassett by one of those men. The eighth item was another action out of character by Orrie Cather. With him present, I told Saul Panzer to see Lucile Ducos and try to learn if she knew anything and if so what, and Orrie suggested that he should see her instead of Saul. It was unheard of for him to suggest that he would be better than Saul for anything whatever. And the next day, last Saturday, came the ninth and last item. Lucile Ducos was shot and killed as she left her home that morning. That was conclusive. It pointed up all the other items, brought them into focus. It was no longer a conjecture that Orrie was implicated; it was a conclusion."

It certainly was a conclusion, the way he told it. Lucile had been killed five days ago. I should have known. We all should have known. I said some chapters back that you probably knew, but, as I also said, you were just reading it and we were in the middle of it. It was like getting the idea that a member of your family had committed three murders. A family affair. Would you have known?

Wolfe was going on. "One more supposition. Suppose that yesterday Archie and Saul, having arrived at the same conclusion, went to that apartment on Fifty-fourth Street and searched the room of Lucile Ducos and found something that your men had failed to find. Hidden in a book on her shelves was a slip of paper on which she had written Orrie Cather's name and address. That made it—"

"By God. I want that. You can't—"

"Pfui. This is supposition. That made it unnecessary for them to spend time and energy seeking further support for their conclusion. They went to Saul's apartment, got Fred to join them, discussed the situation, asked Orrie Cather to come, and when he came they told him how it stood and that they intended, with my help, to make it impossible for him to live. Also they took his gun and kept it."

Wolfe drank coffee and leaned back. "Here reality takes over from invention. This you already know. At half past eleven o'clock this morning Orrie Cather rang my doorbell and was hurtled down to the sidewalk, dead. Evidently he had two of those bombs, since Sergeant Stebbins has told me that scraps of aluminum have been found similar to those found ten days ago on the floor of that room upstairs. Also evidently he didn't wait to see if he would be admitted, because he knew he wouldn't be."

He straightened up and emptied his second cup and reached to put it on the tray. "There's more coffee, still hot, if you would like some. I've finished."

Cramer was staring at him. "And you say you're going to loaf. Drift. It's incredible. *You're* incredible. You're at peace. Good God."

Wolfe nodded. "You haven't had time to consider it from either angle. First your angle. Assume that Orrie Cather is alive and this conversation has not taken place. Where would you stand? Not only would you have no evidence against him; you wouldn't even suspect that he was involved." He turned to me. "What odds would you give that he would never suspect it?"

"A hundred to one. At least."

Back to Cramer. "And you should have. The one item of solid evidence, one that would have been persuasive for a jury, was the slip of paper with Orrie's name on it, which Lucile Ducos had hidden in a book. Your men searched her room and didn't find it. Archie and Saul did find it. You don't know now whether it has been destroyed or is there in my safe. With me, and Archie and Saul and Fred and Orrie, standing mute, you would not only have no evidence, you would have no suspicion. Orrie would be in no jeopardy and almost certainly never would be. In time you would add three to your list of unsolved homicides."

Cramer just sat with his jaw clamped. Of course what really hurt was the slip of paper they had missed. If they had found it— No. I prefer not to put in black and white what it would have been like if they had found it.

"Apparently," Wolfe said, "you don't wish to comment. So much for your angle. Now the other angle—the District Attorney. Orrie Cather is *not* alive. Assume that when you leave here you go to the District Attorney— No, it's past ten o'clock. Assume that in the morning you go to him and report this conversation. Even assume that it is being recorded on a contraption on your person—"

"You know damn well it isn't."

"Assume that it is, and you give it to him. With Orrie Cather dead, what can he do? He can't prefer charges against him, even for three murders. He would of course like to get us, all four of us—have our bail rescinded, lock us up, put us on trial, and convict us. Convict us of what, with us standing mute? Withholding evidence? Evidence of what? Not of murder; no murder will have been legally established. It can't be legally established without someone to charge and convict. Establish a murder by charging us with complicity, and us standing mute? Pfui. Somehow manage to get a report, even a tape recording, of this conversation, into an action of law? Again pfui. I had merely amused myself by inventing a rigmarole of suppositions. I had cozened you."

He turned a palm up. "Being a resourceful man, he could probably pester us, though I don't know exactly how. He has his position and his staff, the power and prestige of his office, but I have resources too. I have ten million people who like to be informed and diverted, and a comfortable relationship with a popular newspaper. If he chooses to try to get satisfaction, I'll try to make him regret it." He turned to me again. "Archie, what odds that we'll have our licenses back before the end of the year?"

I lifted my shoulders and let them down. "Offhand, I'd say twenty to one."

Back to Cramer. "That will be satisfactory for me. I am already in an uncomfortably high tax bracket for the year and would take no jobs anyway. If you want to ask questions about my elaborate supposition, I may answer them."

"I want to ask one. How did she hide the slip of paper in the book? Put it in between the pages?"

"No. She put it on the inside of the back cover, face down, and pasted a sheet of paper over it."

"What's the title of the book?"

"*The Feminine Mystique,* by Betty Friedan. I read about a third of it."

"Where is it?"

Wolfe flipped a hand. "I suppose it has been destroyed."

"Balls. You wouldn't. Wolfe, I want that book. And the slip of paper."

"Mr. Cramer." Wolfe cocked his head. "You haven't reflected. If you reprimand the men who searched that room for misfeasance, whether or not you show them the slip of paper and the book, where will you be? You'll be committed. You will have to report this entire conversation to the District Attorney, of course telling him that you think it was a collection not of suppositions but of facts. You may decide to report it to him anyway, but I doubt it. As I said, your mental processes have limits, but you are not dumb. You would probably be prodded into a long and difficult investigation that couldn't possibly have an adequate result—for instance, you might discover how Mr. Bassett learned Orrie Cather's name and address, but then what? No matter what you discover, even what solid evidence you get, the dominant fact, that Orrie Cather is dead, will remain."

"And you killed him. Your men killed him on your order."

Wolfe nodded. "I won't challenge your right to put it like that. Of course I would put it differently. I might say that the ultimate responsibility for his death rests with the performance of the genes at the instant of his conception, but that could be construed as a rejection of free will, and I do *not* reject it. If it pleases you to say that I killed him, I won't contend. You have worked hard on it for ten days and should have *some* satisfaction."

"Satisfaction my ass." He stood up. "Yes, ten days. I'll reflect on it all right." He went and got his coat and put it on and came back, to the corner of Wolfe's desk, and said, "I'm going home and try to get some sleep. You probably have never had to try to get some sleep. You probably never will."

G 2   He turned, saw the globe, and went and whirled it so hard that it hadn't quite stopped when he was through to the hall. When the sound came of the front door closing, Wolfe said, "Will you bring brandy, Archie? And two glasses. If Fritz is up, bring him and three glasses. We'll try to get some sleep."